"You are a hard ⋯

Shane lifted his gaze ⋯ what he was putting ⋯ inescapable sense that Callie simply wasn't aware of the score, even for all her savvy.

The moment drew out to a taut wire of tension, and all of it sexual.

"What is it you came here for, Callie? I tend to doubt it was me."

She pursed her perfectly sculpted lips into a pout, which was so out of character for her, it actually made him smile. "Darling," she purred, running her thigh along his hip, "don't sell yourself too short. I could be here for you." Her voice was filled with all the carnal knowledge she had of him, making him twitch hard inside his now-snug trousers.

He had carnal knowledge, too. "And I'd certainly never want anything less than complete honesty from you."

Something flashed across her eyes then, so swiftly he'd have missed it if he hadn't been paying close attention. Where Callie was involved, he always paid close attention.

"So noted," she said. "I'm here for two reasons: one, I've gotten wind of your business needs, and two, I simply want you."

"Two tempting offers in one day," he replied.

"Temptation is something we both know more than a little about...."

Blaze™

Dear Reader,

I've come to the end of another series, and it feels both satisfying and sad. Satisfying because I've gotten the opportunity to write about three couples who have taken my writing from relationship stories to sexy romantic suspense. And sad because it's finished. The final novel in my UNDERCOVER LOVERS miniseries is by far the most intense. Callie must remain undercover in her Gina Callahan alias, knowing that at the end of her mission she is going to have to arrest a man she's fallen in love with. As Callie gets closer and closer to him, his facade falls away, and an intricate and fascinating man is revealed. Who is the Ghost and what are his real motivations? Will Callie find out in the end that she's given her heart to friend or foe?

Thank you for taking this journey with me. I so appreciate each and every one of you. I love to hear from readers, so please feel free to e-mail me. May you enjoy this book as much as I enjoyed writing it.

Best,

Karen Anders

Karen Anders

DELICIOUSLY DANGEROUS

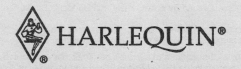

TORONTO • NEW YORK • LONDON
AMSTERDAM • PARIS • SYDNEY • HAMBURG
STOCKHOLM • ATHENS • TOKYO • MILAN • MADRID
PRAGUE • WARSAW • BUDAPEST • AUCKLAND

Recycling programs
for this product may
not exist in your area.

ISBN-13: 978-0-373-79540-6

DELICIOUSLY DANGEROUS

ABOUT THE AUTHOR

Karen Anders is a three-time National Readers' Choice Award finalist and *RT Book Reviews* Reviewers' Choice finalist, and has won the prestigious Holt Medallion. Two of her novels made the Waldenbooks bestseller list in 2003. Published since 1997, she currently writes sexy action/adventure romance for the Harlequin Blaze line. To contact the author please write to her in care of Harlequin Books, 225 Duncan Mill Road, Don Mills, Ontario M3B 3K9, Canada, or visit www.karenanders.com.

Books by Karen Anders

To Tara Cowan for being there
when I needed her

Prologue

JAMMER, AKA THE GHOST, stared out at the mess Max Carpenter and Watchdog had made of Eduardo Fuentes's compound for the second time. All to save one DEA agent, Rio Marshall.

Fuentes was livid. He was an egomaniac and had gotten it into his head that Rio and her FBI bodyguard, Max Carpenter, needed to be eliminated. It didn't look good to Eduardo's Libertad friends that he couldn't keep track of a DEA agent who had eluded him twice. From what Jammer had gleaned in the chase across Maui that had ensued after Max and Rio escaped, Rio had bested Eduardo. Now he wanted her dead more than ever. Although Fuentes's contacts had searched, it was as if the agent and her boyfriend had disappeared off the face of the earth.

But Jammer was pretty sure he could get Fuentes back on track and distract him from his hunt of Rio and Max. The deal Jammer had made to provide a large shipment of weapons to support Fuentes and the paramilitary group the Defensores de la Libertad in their coup of the Colombian government would be front and center again. He'd worked for three years on this deal; he couldn't let anything jeopardize it now that he was so close to the end.

All he had left to do was assemble the rest of the shipment Eduardo required, and for that he'd have to make a trip to some dangerous places and deal with some dangerous people.

Silently, he pulled a picture out of a secret compartment in his wallet. It was a photo of Gina Callahan, the arms dealer he'd met in Paris. He had, for a time, lost himself to her. He still longed to see her, but knew he'd made the right decision in leaving her.

His longing changed into a heavy ache in his chest, but he turned from the window and prepared to calm Fuentes down and move on to the next phase.

Soon it would all be over.

CALLIE CARPENTER STOOD in front of Gillian Santiago, the director of Watchdog. She'd joined the agency only recently, after a stint with the CIA, but she already felt admiration and loyalty for Gillian. Watchdog had taken good care of Callie during her recuperation from the hit-and-run she'd endured while on an undercover mission in Paris. Her assignment had been to hook the Ghost in as a buyer and then, when the deal went down in L.A., take him into custody.

But her twin sister, Allie, had been mistaken for Callie while she'd been decorating Callie's decoy apartment for their birthday, and with Callie out of commission,

Watchdog had recruited both Drew Miller and her tame, interior-designer sister.

Callie had been out of it for most of the two weeks her sister had been posing as her undercover persona, Gina Callahan, a tough-as-nails, spandex-and-tulle-wearing arms dealer. Allie had done a surprisingly good job, but it was Callie's mission and she intended to finish it.

"It says here in your file, Callie, you're fit for duty."

"Yes, ma'am. I'm ready." She was. She'd already made contact with one of the Ghost's lackeys, Jammer. Okay, so it'd been more than simple contact. She'd slept with the guy, unable to resist him. Watchdog didn't know of her personal relationship with Jammer, and once this operation was over, she would have to put him behind bars. She squirmed inside, thinking about how she'd have to use Jammer to get close to the Ghost. But that was what working undercover was all about.

"That's good. Take a look at this." Gillian held out a letter to Callie.

FROM THE OFFICE OF THE PRESIDENT
TOP SECRET AND CONFIDENTIAL
To: Gillian Santiago, Director of Watchdog, Homeland Security
From: The President
It has come to my attention that the fugitive known as the Ghost is still at large. May I remind you the man is a direct threat to national security; he has sold weapons to our enemies. He has murdered government agents, and has broken innumerable national and international

laws. I want this threat eliminated by any means necessary.

Please notify me immediately when he has been either captured or killed.

"The president wants the Ghost dead or alive. That gives us carte blanche, then."

Gillian nodded. "It does, and the perfect opportunity just dropped on my desk. The DEA has just alerted us to the fact that the Defensores de la Libertad in Colombia is throwing their lot in with Eduardo Fuentes."

"Which means they're going to require a shitload of weapons, and for that, they'll need the Ghost," Callie said. It was time to finally put the Ghost out of commission, and if she netted herself a drug lord in the process, well, goody for her.

"All these purchases have been for Fuentes? He's amassing weapons for the Libertad."

"Yes. We believe the weapons you...er, your sister, Allie, sold to the Ghost when she was posing as Tina, your alias Gina Callahan's twin sister, were part of the cache. As are the launchers the Ghost stole from Fudo Miyagi before killing him."

"Miyagi was mine—*I* was the one he wanted dead, or at least he wanted Gina Callahan dead. *I* was the one his thugs ran down in Paris, forcing *my* sister to step in and almost get killed dealing with Miyagi. He was *my* problem."

"You were lucky you survived. And you should be grateful that Jammer took care of *your problem* and helped Drew Miller and Allie to eliminate Miyagi. Jammer double-crossed Miyagi—they had a deal."

"What was the deal?"

"You in exchange for the launchers."

"And instead he betrayed Miyagi, saving me and my sister."

"Do you think that was a deliberate act?" Gillian asked, her tone speculative.

Callie shrugged. "He wanted the launchers, and we know how ruthless the Ghost can be when he wants something. I doubt that he considered his actions would save Allie—or Tina, as he knew her. He most likely instructed Jammer to use her for leverage."

Callie couldn't be sure what "orders" Jammer had received from the Ghost—which had been his decisions and which the Ghost's—but she was sure he had orchestrated it so Miyagi would be on the losing end.

"In any case, now that we know what the Ghost needs, Gina Callahan is going to be very important to this operation."

Callie smiled. "In what way, ma'am?"

"She's going to be in possession of a shitload of weapons."

"I'd better go pack my spandex and tulle."

"DON'T SCREW WITH ME, Igor," Jammer said to the man standing in a warehouse on the outskirts of Minsk. Igor was dressed in a heavy wool coat and wore the requisite *ushanka,* a distinctly Russian hat made out of sheepskin. "You told me you had the weapons I required when I spoke to you last week."

"Then, I did. It is true. But now they are sold." He shrugged. "So sorry. We had no deal. Weapons were, as you say, 'up for grabs.'"

"Son of a—" Jammer paced away from Igor, trying to control his anger, his agitated breath fogging the air. He *needed* those weapons to add to his shipment for Fuentes. Walking back, he said, "A deal was implied, Igor, and you know it."

"*Da,* you make offer. I did not accept. Someone make better offer."

"Who?"

"I do not let this information out of bag. Protecting clients best business. You wish this so, *da?*"

"Yes," Jammer hissed.

"I have more in two weeks. Will this do?"

"No, it won't. I need these weapons yesterday."

Igor shrugged without sympathy. "Market is tight. You will need the good luck to get the amount of weapons you want. Igor cannot help."

"That's just great."

This was a serious setback to his very short deadline. If he didn't deliver as he'd promised, everything he'd worked for would collapse.

Three years of sacrifice would be for nothing.

And that was not acceptable.

1

JAMMER SLAMMED THE DOOR of his hotel room in Minsk, still simmering about the lost opportunity to amass the weapons that Fuentes needed for his deal with the Libertad. He smelled *her* exotic scent and started to turn—a little too late. Someone struck him, knocking his feet out from under him. He hit the carpet hard, the air whooshing out of his lungs. That same someone put a knee into his lower back to keep him immobile.

"Hi, honey, I'm home."

It seemed a lifetime ago since he'd heard that soft, sexy voice. Another kind of simmering overtook him.

"Gina," he said.

"Don't *Gina* me, pal."

He didn't figure Gina for the woman-scorned type, but he could hear the anger in her voice. He had to wonder if he'd gotten to her as much as she'd gotten to him.

"You recovered. Your knee feels like a dagger in my back."

"Just be glad it isn't a real dagger. It would be a shame

to mar such an amazing specimen of muscle and bone. You do have an amazing back…and…front, Jammer. Everything is quite spectacular, in fact."

His body pulsed, remembering how ravenous they'd been for each other. He felt her relax a little. It was the opening he needed, and he took it. Using his superior strength, he pinned *her* to the soft carpet.

Grabbing her wrists as he rolled, he straddled her thighs, using the weight of his body to hold her down.

She didn't fight him or look remotely alarmed. If anything, she looked…excited.

She also looked damn good and a balm to his eyes. She was all black and white, from the cap of mussed black hair with the white streak, to the black-and-white halter top and black mini, to the white stockings and short black stiletto-heeled boots she wore on her feet.

With that combo he thought she should be gracing a stage with her rocker-chick attitude and beautiful, sapphire-blue eyes that showed the world how tough she could be.

He levered his body over hers, tracing his hands down her arms to her delicate wrists. She arched up into him, causing him to swallow a groan of satisfaction as the rigid length of him came into contact with the softest part of her. He managed to find the strength to resist the urge—a primal directive—to drill his hips into hers.

Instead he brought his mouth within a whisper of her lips. "This is a backstabbing business we're in, Gina, but since I don't see a knife in your hand, you must be here for a different reason."

"I am here for something, Jammer. I have an offer for

you." Her lips parted, and she moved sinuously beneath him, torturing them both.

His response was automatic and out of control. Less than ten minutes in her presence and his focus was already shot. He had no business engaging in this activity with Gina. And he didn't give a flat damn. It seemed as if the short number of weeks they'd been apart had been years. He'd waited a long time for a woman like her. Maybe a lifetime.

Too bad it was just too late. For both of them.

His distraction cost him. She bucked her hips and used the momentum to dislodge him and flip him onto his back. This time she weaved her fingers through his, trapping his hands to the carpet.

Their gazes locked. Fused, almost. He half expected the windows to fog up, given how much heat they were generating.

"Is that so?" he said.

She pressed down against his groin, then rubbed along the hardness with abandon. He moaned softly, his eyes closing.

"What do you have to offer me?"

"What? No preliminaries first? No, 'How have you been?' and 'Gee, it's been ages since we've seen each other'?"

"I'd offer you a seat and some fine wine, but I'm a bit indisposed right now."

"I'd forgotten what a charming bastard you are." She smiled then, her eyes twinkling with the mischief he knew all too well. But he had enough brain cells still firing to realize that forgiveness with Gina came at a price. The other reason he liked being close to her was that she kept him on his toes. Even when she was keeping him on his back. An added bonus.

"Now you've hurt my feelings," he said. "I'd hoped you hadn't forgotten a single thing about me." They slipped into their usual banter as if no time had passed. And their playful tête-à-tête was nothing new. Play, however, was something they had more than a little experience in. And playing with Gina was as intoxicating as it was dangerous.

"You, on the other hand, are a hard woman to forget," he said. There was a slight roughness to his tone, one he knew damn well she would pick up on. Just as he knew she'd use every bit of leverage she had with him.

He wished like hell that information bothered him a bit more than it did. He had a shipment to complete and three years of work riding on it; he should bring this to an end and send her packing.

Not entangle himself once again in Gina's very enticing web.

There wasn't a place for her in his world right now—or ever.

"You're not happy to see me. Why is that? Could it be because something big is in the wind?"

It was as if she could read his mind—and he wasn't too certain she couldn't; it would go a long way toward explaining her uncanny ability to stay one step ahead of him. He had to wonder if he had Igor's buyer on top of him right now.

The black leather mini she wore had hiked up in their back-and-forth tussle. He could see the edge of her black garter belt and the tops of her delicate white stockings.

He disengaged his hand, slipping it between them, taking in the way her white stockings made her legs shimmer, the way the lacy band at the top hugged her thighs. Lifting his gaze back to hers, he used his imagination as he traced the garter strap with his fingers, smiled as he touched her panties and her breath quickened. He found the ties at the sides of her hips, and his groin tightened at the thought of how easy it would be to tug on them and remove that flimsy barrier between his fingers and her soft feminine flesh.

"Very, very nice," he murmured, and withdrew his hand from beneath her skirt.

He raised his eyes to hers once more, wondering just what he was putting at risk here. Gina simply wasn't aware of the score, despite her savvy, and that could be dangerous—to his plans and to her. But it might be even more dangerous not to find out what her game was. Besides, all work and no play...

The moment drew out to a taut wire of tension, all of it sexual.

"What is it you came here for, Gina? I tend to doubt it was me."

She pursed her perfectly sculpted lips into a pout, which was so out of character for her it actually made him smile. "Darling," she purred, running her thigh along his hip, "don't sell yourself so short. I *could* be here for you." Her voice was filled with the carnal knowledge she had of him, making him twitch hard inside his now snug trousers.

He fought the urge—a constant battle—to yank her underneath him, shred the black and white covering her, and bury himself so deeply inside her they'd both forget, at least in that instant, why they were really there. He had carnal knowledge, too. And he was sure she'd be wet enough, tight enough, everything enough to fit him perfectly. "And I'd certainly never want anything less than complete honesty from you."

Something flashed across her eyes then, so swiftly he'd have missed it if he hadn't been paying close attention. And, where Gina was involved, he always paid close attention.

"So noted," she said. "I'm here for two reasons. One, I've gotten wind of your need for a lot of weapons, and two, I simply want you."

"Two tempting offers in one day," he replied.

"Temptation is something we both know more than a little about."

SHE'D LOST HER MIND. It was the only explanation.

Two weeks or two years. It wouldn't have mattered. Nothing had changed between them. One grin—one flash of those white teeth—and the calculating professional who always put missions first, self second, vanished. And her inner sex kitten took over. What in the hell did she think she was doing?

She could lie to herself and say she was just doing what she had to in order to get him interested in her offer.

And it would be a lie.

She had never been able to get Jammer out of her

system. Now here he was, still larger than life, still cocky as hell, and pulling her into that same sexual fog she'd barely escaped from last time. She thought she had a handle on it, had the mission fixed firmly in her mind. She was bringing in the Ghost dead or alive. Period.

Without warning, he flipped her onto her back and the air whooshed out of her. If the hit-and-run hadn't put her in the hospital, she half wondered where they would be now. She was no traitor to her country, but she might have warned him to run when he'd had a chance. But she had to contend with the fact that he'd protected her sister, saved her sister's life by double-crossing Miyagi. He had taken the launchers, but instead of turning Allie over to Miyagi, he had helped her and Drew escape, eliminating Miyagi in the process. It made her wonder who he was. Was he the definition of a bad boy—or one of the good guys? Quite an intoxicating mix. And deliciously dangerous. To her, and to her mission.

She moved her hips beneath his, fighting the internal battle of want over need, losing it handily and not particularly caring. He made it easy to play the siren. One look from him and she felt like some untamed elemental whose only mandate was to melt him down to his most basic essence. It was a wonder they both hadn't gone up in flames the last time they tangled.

Which made what she was doing right now the epitome of foolishness.

"I think I'll take you up on one of your propositions," he murmured.

Her entire body shuddered at the mere thought that he wanted more of her. Her head knew it was business.

But tell that to the rest of her. She was in dire need of an edge. More of an edge than the knowledge his raging erection gave her. She hooked her foot around him and rolled him to his back.

She tried to straddle him, but he wrapped his legs around her and kept her fully pinned to him, his fingers still entwined with hers. So much for controlling things.

"On top. That doesn't surprise me. In fact, I think that's where you like to be," he said, his grin resurfacing.

Her pulse doubled. She was in so much trouble. She could shoot the wing off a fly. But she couldn't be around Jammer for more than five seconds without losing every ounce of intellect she possessed. "I don't seem to recall you complaining all that much."

He laughed. "No. No, I didn't." In a maneuver that made her gasp and then smile, he shifted his arms up over his head, locking their fingers, drawing her face closer to his. He abruptly rolled, and she found herself flat on her back again, pinned down by his weight.

She wished it didn't feel so damn good.

There was no pretense now that each of them was trying to restrain the other.

His big hand traveled down her body, and before she could even gasp, his fingers found those tantalizing little ties and released her underwear in one pull. There was nothing in the way of her slick, swollen flesh.

She sucked in a startled breath. Her body grew hot, her skin much too tight and sensitive. Her nipples tingled, and an insistent throbbing gathered low in her belly, between her thighs, the pressure gradually building with every second that passed. She felt sexually charged, feverish and needy in a way she had no power over.

She could feel the heat of his body through his clothes, could inhale how deliciously male he smelled—a heady combination of heat and forbidden passion. His warm breath ruffled the wisps of hair along the side of her face, and pure, undisguised sexual energy crackled between them, a rare and irresistible chemistry that intensified with each moment that passed.

Her body softened, liquefied, automatically readying itself for his possession. No words were spoken—none were needed—as she lifted a hand and curled her fingers around the nape of his neck. She pulled his lips to hers and kissed him deeply, avidly. His mouth was equally burning and eager, his tongue bold and greedy, consuming her with rich, unadulterated pleasure.

She lost control as his mouth grew more demanding, his lips fiery and moist, sliding over hers. She luxuriated in the untamed sensation along with the freedom to do things with and to this man that she'd never explored with another lover before.

He made her feel amazingly feminine and lavishly seductive—as if she were made specifically for him, in every way. And for as long as she was going to be undercover and sticking to him like flies on honey, she *was* his in every way.

Breathing hard and aching for him to touch her, she whispered his name.

Hot, callused hands skimmed down her thighs. Long,

seeking fingers delved into the crease between her legs. She was already wet, already excruciatingly aroused, drunk on passion and the excitement of the forbidden.

She cried out at his touch and his entire body jerked in response. He slanted his mouth across hers again with a rough growl, his tongue thrusting deep.

He found her clit with his thumb and strummed across that knot of nerves in a sleek caress. All it took was that one electrifying touch, and she came in a fast, feverish climax that left her panting and gasping.

Before she could even get air into her lungs, he rose up off the floor in one powerful move that made her lose her breath all over again. It wasn't far to the bed, thank you very much.

Night had fallen and as he got closer to the bed he was silhouetted against the glow of the city lights through the window.

Her entire body hummed in anticipation. Not that she could really fault her reaction; of course it was going to hum a little. Okay, a lot. But she wished she could stay focused on more important things than what Jammer could do with his very impressive body.

Like how she was going to keep her cool around this man long enough to get close to the Ghost. How was she going to handle it when she had to put cuffs on Jammer and turn him over to the court system to be tried—a trial she would have to testify at to put both Jammer and the Ghost away?

Once he knew she was Callie Carpenter, a Watchdog agent sent here to discover the identity of his boss and arrest them both, this delicious *thing* between them would be over.

She'd have to be disgusted with herself later.

"You smell incredible," he said as he let her slide down his fully aroused, heavily muscled frame.

Much later.

Her face was closer to his, his own smell intoxicating. Her knees went decidedly wobbly, and she knew she should be ashamed at how easily he could seduce her into putting everything important in her world on hold. But damn the man, he made it really hard to concentrate. And it wasn't like there was anything she could do to further the investigation in the next fifteen minutes, anyway. Or the next hour. Or two.

Or three.

"So it's clear which proposition you intend to take, but couldn't it be an all-inclusive deal?"

"Business is important, Gina, but I have some investigations of my own to conduct, right here and right now. Fuck, I missed you."

"I'm serious about the offer, Jammer." The reprimand was aimed more at herself than him. But if she hoped to enlist some of his control in the matter she was going to be sorely disappointed. Except disappointment wasn't really what she was feeling at all when his eyes went dark and he reached up and released the strings on her halter top.

"What you do to me," he murmured as he walked her backward toward the bed, without ever once actually touching her, but staying so deep in her personal space she felt intimately connected to him.

"If you're trying to distract me, that's not a bad way to go," she said, hearing the thread of need in her voice, even as she tried valiantly to keep from slipping under his spell without a sign of struggle. He wouldn't be around long, and she was warring between giving in to her inner sex kitten, which was purring for indulgence, and preserving some sense of willpower over wanting too much. Certainly she would end up wanting more than she was ever able to keep.

His only response was to slip out of his suit coat, loosen his tie and unbutton his starched white shirt to reveal a chest that was fashioned by the gods for women to worship.

"Jammer? Throw me a bone," she said, although the words weren't much more than a hushed whisper as he leaned in and slid the zipper of her mini down.

"How about a boner?"

She laughed and her breasts brushed his chest, her nipples tightening into hard, taut peaks begging for more.

His face tightened into hot sexual hunger, his eyes zeroing in on her breasts. He grabbed her around the waist. Sliding her skirt off, he lifted her, his biceps bunching into rock-solid knots of power.

He pressed his lips to one aching, tingling crest and opened his mouth over it. He sucked, and she felt the tugging, pulling sensation all the way down to her sex. She couldn't stop the whimper of need that escaped her lips. She braced herself on the concrete bulges of his biceps, her head dropping back as he shifted and took her other throbbing nipple into his mouth to suckle.

She shuddered and held on to his arms, her need for him becoming a tangible thing, strong and powerful and nearly devastating in its intensity.

He lowered her to the floor and reached for his belt buckle. It wasn't until he started pushing his pants off his hips that a self-satisfied smile tugged at the corners of his mouth. "You're talking way too much about business, Gina."

"I'm just trying…" She'd been so caught up in watching, she'd forgotten what she was going to say. "Oh, never mind." She sighed, smiling herself, shamelessly enjoying the rest of Jammer naked.

He tugged the halter off, undid the garter belt and slowly rolled the stockings down her legs, which put him in a convenient crouch in front of her. She let out a gasp and balanced herself by gripping his strong shoulders as he took a wicked detour with his tongue. "We're so completely shameless," she groaned.

"A beautiful thing, wouldn't you say?"

"Yeah," she said, torn between a laugh at how freeing it was to be with him, and a quiet moan at how deliciously good the things he was doing with his tongue made her feel. The soft moan won as he continued his very focused, tender assault on her most sensitive little bundle of nerve endings. "It's overwhelming. Have I mentioned that your foreplay technique is more than I can resist?" She groaned when he slid his tongue away from the place she wanted him to be, up over her stomach, gasping again when he captured one erect nipple for a brief, luscious moment, then moved up to kiss her neck. "You stopped," she said, pouting just a little.

"I hate doing the expected," Jammer said with a twinkle in his eyes. "That gets boring."

"I'll have to remember to keep my big trap closed."

2

"I LIKE YOUR BIG TRAP just the way it is," he said, "Clever mouth and all."

"Clever mouth?" she asked with a tiny smile that spoke volumes. With all her might she reared up, her hands planted firmly on his oh-so-broad shoulders. She startled him, and when he landed flat on his back on the bed with her straddling him, he laughed out loud.

Callie felt every inch of his erection, and every inch of her throbbed from the inside out.

Without warning, she covered his mouth in a swoop of heat and put every seductive nuance into it. She teased, withdrawing and making him chase her, then erotically licking the line of his lips before she pushed her tongue between. A hot, desperate need went down to her pores as she kissed him. When she broke the kiss, she smoothed both palms over his skin and dragged her tongue across his nipple, then suckled.

He groaned deep in his chest, his body trembling beneath hers. He gripped her hips, wedging closer. His hand slid upward, along her ribs, teasing the underside of her breasts, cupping her and massaging her engorged nipples.

"You certainly aren't predictable, Gina."

Her lips quirked. "I would rather not be remembered as being boring. When you think about me down the road, I want you to smile."

"Ah, you're not going to be like Cinderella and leave the ball too soon, are you?"

"Cinderella? I'm no one's lackey."

"Of course not. Didn't mean it that way."

"What did you mean?"

"The prince was so in the dark about who she really was. To him, she was mystery and intrigue. So much so, he had to find her and make her his."

She looked away, hearing way too much meaning in his voice, the slant of his mouth, the banked need in his eyes. She didn't know what her eyes would give away at that moment, but she didn't dare risk it. So she went for flirtation, dropping further into her Gina persona to hide the feelings that Callie harbored for this man—a man she was planning on destroying.

"Awww, does the prince need a plaything for just a little bit longer?"

"Mmm-hmm, and he has a glass slipper he wants to try on for size."

She breathed a mental sigh of relief when he moved with her into this lighter, teasing banter. It allowed her distance—and distance with this man was the only thing that was going to save her from falling under his very seductive spell.

"From this vantage point, I think it might be just a

mite too big. Maybe it'll fit the ugly stepsister." It took all her willpower to lie on his hot, muscled body and chitchat with him as if the volatile energy between them wasn't jolting every atom and air particle in the room.

His laugh was deep and genuine as it vibrated through her torso.

"No, I think this slipper was custom-made for you." She felt his stomach muscles ridge like sculpted granite as he bowed toward her and latched on to her nipple, giving it a nip. She groaned softly.

Then he suckled her once more, his mouth warm, wet and skilled. Her hips moved in restless thrusts against his pulsing groin.

She slid down his body, slow and gradual, alternately tasting him with her tongue and kissing his smooth chest, down his rigidly defined abdomen and across all his taut, honey-toned skin to his groin. "I'll have to check out this glass slipper for myself," she breathed, and he moaned.

But there was nothing transparent or fragile about him or his…slipper.

Jammer was a big man, broad through the shoulders, thick through the chest. He looked like he belonged in a bar, in the role of bouncer, or in the ring as a larger-than-life wrestler.

And the man was more well endowed than Callie had ever seen. He knew how to fill a woman up.

"What are you doing down there?"

She chuckled. "Admiration comes to mind. Hey, aren't you supposed to be charming?"

"Are you kidding? With you keeping me on erotic tenterhooks, how am I—"

She chose that moment to take him fully and deeply into her mouth, and his words were cut off in a sensual gasp.

He was hot and pulsing in her mouth as she curled her fingers around the base of his cock and sucked.

"You're killing me, woman."

She licked and sucked her way to the head of his erection, and Jammer moved his hips restlessly. She looked up at him, to find his eyes riveted on her, filled with a pleasure that transcended the word. And…something more. Something that Callie didn't want to see and was sure Jammer hadn't wanted to reveal as his eyes shuttered and he closed them.

A woman's power over a man in this situation was absolute. She should exploit it, but the reluctance to use him in any way was so firmly ingrained, she couldn't do it. She knew he worked for a ruthless gunrunner, one who had wreaked havoc on more than one agent from more than one agency, but Jammer was different from the Ghost. He had integrity.

He'd saved Allie's life and he'd also had a hand in rescuing her brother Max's new love, DEA agent Rio Marshall, from Fuentes's stronghold in Hawaii. Max had received a phone call from the Ghost telling him exactly where he could find Rio, but Callie suspected it hadn't been the Ghost who had made that call. Were the reasons for what Jammer had done altruistic or just a means to further his own plans? Callie didn't have the answer.

She worked him hard and brought him closer and closer to orgasm.

But she didn't get the chance. He grabbed her under the arms and jerked her up his body, his eyes alight with a fire and a desire that consumed her.

PURE HEAT AND WILD HUNGER. The power of it sped down his body and fought for escape. Instead, it built, a need like sucking in a lungful of air that wouldn't come. It almost scared him, opened up feelings he'd buried so he could do what he had to—but fighting it was impossible. Gina made him *feel*. Just by her very existence. She was her own adventure, her own ruler, and the thrills of putting together a high-risk buy didn't compare to the ecstasy of Gina naked and pressed against him, her mouth moving savagely over his.

His hands swept up her tight ribs, cupping her breasts, and the contact was electric, her kiss stronger, hurried. He thumbed her nipples in slow circles, and her shudder tumbled into his mouth. Strong thighs clamped him and he broke the kiss and held her gaze as he bent her over his arm and closed his lips on her nipple.

She threw her head back, moaning beautifully, then watched him take her deep into the heat of his mouth. "Now you're being more than charming," she breathed.

He smiled against her skin, lifting her higher, his tongue sliding wetly over her breasts, his teeth deliciously scoring the plump underside. But it wasn't enough. He wanted her screaming. He wanted her weak and panting and vulnerable—only for him.

Her fingers dug into his shoulder. "Now, right now, Jammer."

"Nope."

"Killjoy."

He smiled, then grimaced as she skimmed her hand over his rock-hard erection. He was a man who prided himself on his staying ability, but Gina was sorely testing him. The pleasure that rippled up through him from her clever fingers blindsided him.

His erection flexed in her hand. "Now you're killing me," she said. She pushed his penis down, gliding wetly across him, teasing him.

"Now that would be impossible, because you're so alive!" He tossed her on her back, grabbing the headboard and thrusting into her. He left her completely and slid back, loving the flare in her blue eyes, the smile that never seemed to fade.

She reached up and smoothed her fingers over his jaw, let them flutter down his body as he plunged into her once more.

It didn't get more erotic than this, he thought, and then she proved him wrong. She locked her legs around him, her hands on his chest as she shoved him back, never stopping. Her hips curled in a rhythmic wave, letting him feel every inch of his erection sliding in her. For a moment Jammer was mesmerized by her stomach muscles contracting, her spine bending and pushing her hips into his. His hands closed over her breasts, thumbs circling slowly, and her eyelids lowered, their tempo increasing with her breathing.

He let her keep control. She seemed to need it. She

gripped his arms, holding on and riding, faster and harder. She called his name, an expression almost like fear in her eyes. Jammer cupped the back of her head, forced her to look directly at him as his fingers skated over the bead of her sex. Her eyes glazed.

"More, please more," she whispered, and he laid her down and hammered into her, felt the claw of her body on his, the rage of passion sweeping over him. He was uncontrollable with the mindless need to drive harder, and their momentum pushed her across the bed.

Yet she matched him, her hips pistoned to his. Then his world split, his climax burst, and she gripped him, moving faster as his body tightened and rocketed with exploding thrusts.

Gina arched, her spine bending so far he thought she'd snap. She clutched his hips, grinding him into her. "Kiss me, now."

It was a primal directive and he took her lips like a man starving. She came, her scream muffled and shuddering into his mouth, her molten core jerking. He slammed into her, the rip of pleasure tearing over his skin, pulsing with her. They strained, held on, and let the sweep of it take them.

Jammer groaned, the waves of pure ecstasy crackling though him. She collapsed on the bed, and he'd barely caught his breath when she said, "I guess that slipper fit, after all."

He chuckled and looked at her. Gina touched his face, pulled him down on her, and he rolled with her to his side, drawing her leg over his. For a long moment they just stared, damp, a tangle of legs and arms.

"You're under my skin, Cinderella."

Her eyes danced with a snappy comeback, but instead, she said, "Anywhere near your skin is fine with me."

He leaned in and rubbed his mouth softly over hers. She snuggled closer, her eyes still caught in his.

"Think the whole hotel heard us?"

"Do you care?"

"There's little that could embarrass me, Jammer." She shifted on top of him, and Jammer reveled in her soft, lush, completely sexy body on his, sweeping his hand up her behind. They stayed like that, sinking into the sensations, the tenderness, then Gina braced her arms on his chest, her chin on her hands. He smiled.

"Let me know when you're ready to do that again."

Jammer laughed, clamping his arms around her and flipping her to her back. "No time like the present." With his knee, he nudged her thighs wide.

"Ah, now you're just showing off."

A HALF AN HOUR LATER, his cell phone rang.

"There better be coffee on the other end of the line," Gina said sleepily.

"I'm going to beat the hell out of whoever's calling," Jammer groused, reaching down and snagging his pants.

"Don't answer it," she muttered.

"I have to." He smoothed his hand through her hair. "I've got too many irons in the fire."

"I like the way you use your iron and your fire...."

Her voice faded as he glanced over. She was sprawled

on the bed, half-asleep, every inch of her beautiful skin exposed. The ring came again, incessant and jangling.

"This had better be good," he snapped into the phone.

"Sorry to bother you, boss, but I've done as you asked, contacted everyone you told me to contact. There just aren't any weapons out there for purchase. Not the kind we need or the volume."

"Talk to Romanoff. See what he's got."

Jammer ended the call and swore softly under his breath.

"What's wrong?"

He said nothing. He wasn't going to drag her into his business. She could screw up this deal, a deal he'd staked his career and his life on. The situation was too dangerous and too volatile, and he liked Gina alive. *Damned* alive, as a matter of fact, especially when she melted all over him like warm chocolate. She had to get away from the shit before it hit the fan, because when it did, it was going to be ugly.

"Okay, be silent and deadly," she said.

He rose and got dressed, and Gina watched him with her bright blue eyes.

"Your contacts have dried up. You've called everyone you know and there are no weapons to be found. You need a big, big shipment, but you're already behind deadline and you're getting pressure from the man who wants those weapons. He's not being all that patient. You're in a bad bind. You need me."

In more ways than one. Another reason why he had to shut her out. "Think you're pretty slick, slick?"

She rose and he got lost in all those moving curves and jiggles. She sat on the edge of the bed totally naked and crossed her legs as if she was at a garden party social.

"The way I see it you need my help, and I'm more than willing to cash in on this deal." Her tone turned serious. With gunrunners, weapon buys were always serious.

But it reminded him of why she was really here— another twist in an already intricate maze that was his life.

"Yeah, because the deal we put together last time went so well."

"That wasn't your fault, Jammer. But you made sure it worked out in our favor."

"I hated leaving your sister and her right-hand guy holding the bag."

"You didn't. My sister is very resourceful." Callie couldn't believe how resourceful Allie had been. She was extremely proud of her. Allie had been a tame interior designer when Drew Miller had mistaken her for Callie. Then he had embroiled her twin sister in an undercover mission, where she had posed as "Tina" to complete the deal Gina had made with Jammer in Paris before the hit-and-run had taken her out of commission. Despite the scare with Miyagi, it had turned out well, and Drew and Allie were now completely in love.

"Good, you got your cut."

"I always get my cut."

"Then you understand when I say that I have a business to run."

"Right." She rose and started to dress. As she pulled up and zipped her skirt, she turned to search for her boots. He was standing there with them in his fist.

She snatched the boots out of his hand and put them on. "It was always about the weapons, as it should be," she said, turning her back to him. "Miyagi was my own personal problem."

She marched to the door. "Look, I'm not one to push my services on anyone. If you don't want to talk shop, I'm outta here."

He grabbed her wrist and pulled her around. His gaze locked on hers, so intent, so focused.

"Gina," he whispered, bringing his forehead near hers, his face inches away. "Surely you've got to know. I did it all for you. He was a man without a soul and an abuser and an enslaver of women. He tried to kill you, and for that he had to die. He got what he deserved."

She was speechless and touched by this man who'd orchestrated the death of a monster who would have stopped at nothing to see her dead. It cut into her defenses—the defenses she needed to keep him at arm's length. Standing this close, looking into his eyes, she saw no sign of deception, no wavering. He was either being completely honest and open to her at this moment or he was a really good actor.

"That's hitting below the belt, Jammer." Her voice was wobbling, but he'd have had that effect on her even if she wasn't hanging by a thread.

"No, it's not. Do you have any idea how hard it was to walk away from you in the hospital when you were injured?"

"But you did."

"Yes, I did, because it was better for me and for you. I've got something to do and it encompasses everything that I am. I'm walking a fine line and it's a fucking dangerous one. I don't want you on it. I cannot afford distractions and complications."

"So you're saying I'm both."

"You are a big pain in the ass, Gina, and you know it."

She laughed out loud because she did know it. She was too much of a smart aleck for her own good.

She wished she could be the one to walk away from him, but Watchdog had given her a mission and she was going to follow through on it. She was confident that Jammer wouldn't find the weapons he was so desperate for without her.

"Okay, fine. It's been a slice. I'll see you around." She looked at him, so steady, so strong-willed, so profoundly sure of himself. So very sure of her. And if she did her job, that would be his downfall.

She slowly extricated herself from his hand. This time he let her go. And, perversely, her heart fell.

His phone started to ring as she grabbed the door-knob. She got a lot of satisfaction in slamming the door as she left.

But that didn't last long. Once in her own room, she started to pack. She would have to make it appear as if she was going, but she had no intention of letting this mission fail. The Ghost was as good as caught.

She whipped off her clothes and took a hot shower. She quickly dried herself off, squeezing the water out of her hair before running a comb through it. She slipped on a white silk robe with butterflies fluttering all over it.

Sitting down on the edge of the bed, she thought about how to hedge her bets. There was a time to give up and a time to fight. If she wanted to get to the Ghost, she was going to have to make sure that she was the only one with all the neat, cool toys.

She picked up the phone she used as Gina and dialed. When the voice answered at the other end, Callie said, "This is Gina Callahan. Let me speak to Reggie."

But before her contact came on the phone, there was a quick, hard knock on her door. She told the guy that she would have to call him back, and then severed the connection.

When she pulled the door open, she did nothing to make it any easier for Jammer.

"Want a drink?" she asked, a smug smile drifting across her face.

With his stormy eyes and tight jaw he looked so dangerous that she swallowed. But her persona never wavered. Stepping away from the door with a nonchalance she didn't feel, she walked over to the mini-bar, poured herself three fingers of vodka and downed it.

She sensed his presence behind her. He was like an inferno at her back. She felt the gentle stroke of his fingers down the smooth fabric of her silk robe.

"Let's talk about the ground rules," she said.

He laughed softly and turned her around. "There are no ground rules, Gina. I make the plans and you follow through. It'll be fifty-fifty, just like last time. I have the buyer and you have the contacts. When I have what I need, we part company. Deal?"

He'd changed and showered, too, his hair a gorgeous spiked disarray. He smelled delicious and male. The baby-blue sweater and tight blue jeans all looked good on his heavily muscled body.

"Deal," she said.

"This is easy for you, isn't it? Just another deal in the many you've put together. Don't you get tired of it?"

His questions and serious tone caught her off guard. Something about the morning beard shadowing his jaw, the way his hair wasn't quite so naturally perfect, made his eyes darker and enhanced how impossibly thick his eyelashes were. And she really, really needed to stop focusing on his mouth. But the ruggedness the stubble lent to his face just emphasized those soft, sculpted lips of his.

Tired of playing the espionage game? Maybe a little, and maybe even more when she thought about how she'd have to put this man behind bars for the rest of his life. He wouldn't soon forgive her for that. Gina Callahan was a role, and most undercover people would say that you couldn't play at undercover. A persona must be lived, not adopted, or your identity would soon be given away.

But there was something so open and sincere in Jammer's face that Callie couldn't seem to get out the off-the-cuff words Gina would have said.

"Not when I deal so damn well," she said, finally dodging that odd feeling that Jammer was looking right through her masquerade and seeing her, Callie Carpenter, peering out.

But that wasn't possible, or they wouldn't be having this conversation at all. Callie wasn't under any illusion that if Jammer even suspected who she was he would come anywhere near her. What he had going with Fuentes was going to pay out big, and she was sure the Ghost wanted his score.

But this time Callie was going to be ready to nab him and fulfill her mission, a mission that had foiled more than one operative before her.

Jammer seemed disappointed in her answer and stepped forward. "You're not tired of constantly looking over your shoulder? Wondering if the next deal is going to be the last? Giving up so damn much?"

She didn't know what to say. She hadn't expected this from him; each time she was with the man she found a different, more fascinating facet to him. He wasn't a muscle-bound lackey at all, but an intelligent, forceful personality that kept her constantly on her toes.

"Jammer," she said softly, reaching out to touch his face, his stubble rough against her palm.

He moved in closer, crowding her against the wall, his big body trapping her. Why couldn't she resist him?

Because the sexual tension hadn't abated one whit. But also, she told herself, because she *could* give in to him—commitment had nothing to do with lust. She could be as lustful as she wanted, crave his touch, want to know what he tasted like, felt like…and have absolutely no intention of settling into a relationship with him. She had a job to do.

Circumstances being what they were, she could be forgiven for simply taking what she could have.

Him.

The silence expanded in a way that lent texture to the very air between them. He was so warm, the temperature rose a considerable notch.

"What do you want me to say? I don't know—"

He buried his face in the crook of her neck and shoulder and sighed deeply. "Don't say anything. It really won't make a difference."

He raised his head. His lips curved then, and her thighs—or more accurately, the muscles between them—suddenly felt a whole lot more wobbly.

His eyes were so dark, so deep, she swore she could fall right into them and never climb back out. And that part sad, part whimsical smile made it dizzyingly clear that Jammer was more than physically dangerous.

She was a trained operative, trained for all aspects of the clandestine job she performed, but Callie found the compassion she felt for people was a detriment. Like what had happened with Miyagi, a man whom she had originally tracked down—on her own and without the agency's knowledge—because she'd empathized with another man, Jason Kyoto, who was trying to rescue his sister from Miyagi and a life of forced sexual slavery, and she'd vowed to help him. She'd gone rogue from Watchdog for just a short period of time. Sure, she'd made an enemy of Miyagi and almost got herself and Allie killed because of it, but she'd fulfilled her mission and saved Jason's sister.

So it was disconcerting that the same compassion

she'd felt was once again going to get her in hot water unless she resisted the impulse.

"What brought all these questions on?"

He lifted his hand, barely brushing the underside of her chin with his fingertips, and tipped her head back a bit farther.

"I think about you," he said, his voice nothing more than a rough whisper.

Her skin tingled as if the words themselves had brushed against her.

"Too often. You distract me."

"And that's a bad thing?"

"It's…an unexpected thing," he said.

"I hear you. In our business distractions can get us killed."

"Bingo," he said. He smiled.

"Getting this close to me is going to help in some way? Although you won't hear me complaining."

His smile broadened as his mouth lowered slowly toward hers. "Either that, or make all this distraction a lot more worthwhile. Let's seal our deal with a kiss."

It was never a question of not meeting his lips. Her body was fairly humming in anticipation and it was all she could do to refrain from grabbing his head and hurrying him the hell up.

It was just a kiss and a contract.

His lips brushed across hers. Warm, a little soft, but the right amount of firm. He slid his fingers along the back of her neck, beneath the hair on her nape, sending a delicious little shiver all the way down her spine.

He dropped another whisper of a kiss across her lips,

then another, inviting her to participate, clearly not going any further unless she did. She respected that, a lot, even though part of her wished he'd taken the decision out of her hands. It would make all the self-castigation later much easier to avoid. Given his aversion to commitment, somehow she figured he knew that. They were either in it together or not at all.

She held his gaze for what felt like an eternity, and then slowly lowered her eyelids as she closed the distance between them and returned his kiss.

His fingers fluttered against the back of her neck when she opened her mouth on his, then pressed a bit harder as he accepted her compliance and nipped her bottom lip with a sensual tug before deepening the kiss.

She had no defense against this, against him. It was too delectable, and he was impossible to resist. Especially when she didn't really want the contact to end. She shut out thoughts of what would happen next, and tried hard, very hard, to just enjoy this for as long as it lasted.

He pulled away. "Get packed. I've booked us for the States and the plane leaves in three hours."

Then he was slipping out the door. Her mouth still tingled as she slumped against the wall. The door hadn't fully closed when he leaned back inside and gave her a bad-boy smile.

"Get going," he barked, and she flipped him the bird, but he only laughed.

3

THE LONG FLIGHT FROM Minsk put them into San Francisco just before dawn, and as they drove into St. Helena the sun was rising over the countryside, showcasing beautiful green vineyards, oak-lined streets and antique hotels. Callie saw a lot of activity for so early in the morning, but September in Napa was no time to rest, as it was the beginning of the grape harvest.

After they passed through the quaint town of St. Helena, Jammer turned off onto a road that led to a stone castle estate with lush vineyards nestled in the rolling hills beyond. The sign out front read Ceo Draiochta.

"What language is that? Gaelic? Do you have Scottish ancestry?" Callie angled around to look at him.

He made a faint curl of his mouth, not quite a smile. He seemed remote, somewhere far beyond her in his thoughts, even though he was only two feet away. "It's Gaelic and my background…is complicated."

"What does it mean?" she asked.

"Magic Mist."

"Ah, how pretty. For the fog that blankets these

hills?" Callie had seen plenty of photos of Napa Valley obscured by thick fog.

"Yes, reminiscent of the hills of Scotland with their mysterious mists," he said.

"Hmm, very poetic, I'd say."

"The fog is legendary here. It rolls up the valley or makes its way through the gaps between the Mayacamas from neighboring Sonoma Valley. There are days when I wake up and find the valley 'was gone; gone were all the lower slopes and the woody foothills of the range; and in their place, not a thousand feet below me, rolled a great level ocean.'"

"Robert Louis Stevenson?"

"I'm impressed," Jammer said.

"So am I. There aren't many gunrunners I know who can quote Stevenson. He was, if I'm not mistaken, a Scottish poet and writer."

"You aren't mistaken," he growled.

"Hmm, a pattern here."

"I would ask that you be cautious of what you say in front of my staff. They don't know anything about what I really do. They run the winery for me and are good people."

"Are you changing the subject?"

"Moving on to a different one, that's all."

"So, this is a legit business?"

"Yes. I make some of the best cherry brandy and cabernet sauvignon on the market—Craving Cherry Brandy, Brume Reserve, Chimera Estate and Tempest Estate."

"What name do you go by here?"

"They only know me as Mr. J. I have a manager who handles the staff, since I travel a lot."

They pulled into a circular paved driveway with a beautiful fountain in the middle and luscious blooms of a wide variety of flowers in a kaleidoscope of shades, all bracketed by verdant greenery.

Then Callie examined the house. It was a castle complete with turrets. "Okay, you're taking this Scottish theme to the max."

He laughed as he exited the car.

"Does it have a dungeon?"

"Yes, and if you don't stop asking questions, I'm going to put you on the rack."

"Oooh, that sounds way too good. Will you ravish me while I'm helpless?"

"Most decidedly. If only to stop you from talking."

His gaze slid down her body, touching every part of her with a hot, melting look. Her face, her shoulders, her breasts. She licked dry lips and could almost taste him on them.

He stepped closer to her, that mouth a sensual line of taut beauty. When he captured her lips, she got a thrill of sensation at the feel of his oh-so-soft and oh-so-clever mouth. It was a kiss meant to tease and to tantalize, ending much too quickly.

"Hey, I was just doing as I was told," he said.

She sighed deeply. "Oh, yes, that's right. I told you to remind me to keep my big trap shut. Thanks for that."

He slipped his hand into hers and Callie started at the contact. It seemed more intimate than the kiss they had just shared and more dangerous than the mission she was on.

He pulled her forward onto the small drawbridge that served as the front path to the winery grounds and the castle beyond. A riot of color surrounded them on the short walk.

The house itself was made of stone and included a round tower on its side, making it look truly like a castle.

"The tasting rooms and the winery production is done in those old barns over there," he said, pointing to the right of the house.

"Not really old, huh?"

"No, just manufactured to look that way."

"This is an interesting side of you. A legitimate businessman."

"I have many identities, Gina. This is just one of them."

"I can't imagine how you manage to do your...ah... gunrunning right under these people's noses."

"I don't do that kind of business here."

"What do you mean?"

"No one from that world knows about this place. Well, except for Fudo Miyagi and he's dead. He was also escorted here without foreknowledge."

"Why would you bring that man here, to your sanctuary?"

"To garner his trust and put him at ease. It's a beautiful place."

"But you brought *me* here. Does that mean I have to die, too?"

He turned to her, his eyes unreadable. "I wanted us to be untraceable during this deal we have going. I don't want to entertain any surprises. After all, you have the contacts and I need those. Your welfare is my main concern."

"Just like you took care of my sister?"

"More," he said.

He drew her forward again, to the carved mahogany doors. Over the curved archway was a polished coat of arms. More show.

They stepped into a cool foyer, the floor a polished slate gray, the walls a darker gray.

The great room was furnished in deep blues and greens, with comfy sofas and warm wood tables, drawing an appreciative sigh from her. More facets to an already fascinating man.

They passed a large dining room and staircase that led, she presumed, to the second level and the bedrooms, before making their way into the gleaming, state-of-the-art kitchen.

"Thirsty?"

"Yes, very."

He dropped her hand and opened a massive double-door refrigerator, selecting two bottles of sparkling water and handing her one. He opened the other and took a long pull, his throat muscles working.

Callie twisted the top off her bottle and took a sip. She tugged out a chair near the island and sat down, the fatigue of the trip and the sheer act of maintaining her undercover persona catching up with her.

"You're tired. Let me—"

A sudden knock on the door interrupted him, and he went to answer it. Callie could hear a male voice and Jammer's deep tones responding. He came back into the kitchen, accompanied by a tall man with a shock of black hair. The newcomer stopped short, his eyes widening as he scanned her sleeveless, pink cotton shirt, which fit like a second skin. That was where the sugar-and-spice-and-everything-nice ended. Her many-shades-of-green camo miniskirt hugged her hips and was belted with chain mail. Black tights covered her legs, ending at stiletto-heeled combat boots on her feet. She knew she looked like Lara Croft ready to do battle.

Callie laughed softly and slipped off the stool. Walking over to Jammer's employee, she curled her index finger under his chin and closed his gaping mouth.

"Gina, don't harass the help."

"Oh, but it's so much fun."

"I'm sorry, Mr. J. Didn't realize you had company." The man looked at her sheepishly and then smiled through his embarrassment, rubbing at the blush on his cheeks.

"It's no problem, Jim. This is Gina Callahan. She's going to be staying with us for a few days."

"That's great, Mr. J. She'll get a chance to see a working winery and taste some of our finest wines."

"Jim was just letting me know that there are some matters that need my attention. Boring for you, Gina." Jammer turned to Jim. "I'll just take her upstairs and get her settled. Could you get her bags out of the car?"

"Sure."

"Come on, sleepy, let's get you to bed."

"All by my lonesome?" She pouted.

Jammer shifted closer, lowering his head slightly so she had to tilt her chin to maintain eye contact. "For now. I've got to take care of business, and then I'll give you a tour."

On the way up the stairs, she glimpsed a study. The door was partially open, revealing shelves full of books, a desk and a laptop computer on top.

She'd do well to see what was on the laptop, hopefully find out information Gillian could use.

But Callie's attention was immediately diverted by Jammer's firm butt in those heavenly jeans he was wearing. If she didn't need the time to snoop…she'd make sure he ended up in bed with her. But she had to focus on why she was really here—and it wasn't for a wine-filled Napa Valley vacation.

She was here to nab the Ghost, and she intended to do it.

True to his word, he took her to a charming master suite complete with a big inviting bed, whirlpool tub and a huge shower decked out with more showerheads and nozzles than she'd ever seen.

"Have a good nap and I'll see you when you wake up," he said, ready to turn and leave.

"We'll talk strategy?"

"That was the plan."

"I know that. I don't have any expectations."

"A woman like you who does this kind of a thing for a living never does, right?"

The way he said the words made her inner agent stand at attention. And that made her uneasy. *She* controlled the situation in her undercover operations, always. But this time, from the moment she had met him, he'd been at the head of the line and she had to wonder why that was the case. He seemed to know what she was thinking, but the expression was gone in an instant.

His big hand came up and caressed her neck. It would have been nothing for him to tighten it and choke the life out of her. But his fingers were gentle against her.

The attraction was there, pulling at her every time he looked at her. Strong, magnetic, beyond her control. And that made her uneasy all over again. He was trouble. A man with secrets in his eyes and a dark side he took great pains to camouflage. A man whose baser instincts ran just beneath the surface. Dangerous. She'd thought so more than once.

But it was as if she was addicted to him, to the danger he embodied. She couldn't be sure. All she knew was that she was hip deep in alligators and they had razor-sharp teeth. Especially if he suspected her true identity.

But she was certain he would protect his boss with deadly force, so he couldn't be suspicious of who she really was, or he would have killed her a long time ago.

Unless he was expecting to get something out of her. But what could that be? Of course, she did have something of great value to him—her contacts.

He got that distant look in his eyes again as if he was miles away, and she had to wonder what he was thinking. And who he really was, this man who gave her so much pleasure, tantalized her senses and made her feel so alive.

A man she would have to destroy to fulfill her mission.

He trailed the back of his hand up her neck to the side of her face and sighed. "You make me want to forget about everything, but that's not possible."

"No," she agreed. "We both have a mission to accomplish."

His eyes darkened slightly, and his smile hardened. "Interesting choice of words."

She instantly wanted to bite her lip, frantically going over everything she'd said to him. He was standing entirely too close, so she was missing whatever it was he'd picked up on. She decided to play it cool even though she was feeling nothing of the sort. "Mixing business and pleasure can sometimes be a volatile combination. Don't you agree?"

"As long as one doesn't interfere with the other, it will work out fine for both of us."

"I'm not some wide-eyed innocent. I know the score. All's fair in love and war."

"No, it isn't. If things were fair," he said, "we wouldn't be attracted to each other in the first place." He crowded her the tiniest bit nearer to the wall. "We'd never have gotten entangled." He shifted a bit more. She didn't stop him. "If things were fair, I'd have never gone to that hotel room in Paris and we would never have met."

Her heart was beating so hard now she couldn't even hear herself speak.

"Ah, Gina, if we were different people and this was a different situation, there would be no holding back."

"Oh, Jammer. We are who we are."

"Yes, with all those complications. Even though I want more, we will have to do with less."

Of all the things he could have said, he'd chosen the one guaranteed to raise every defensive wall she could construct. She could never allow herself to be exposed in any way—and what he wanted from her would definitely qualify as exposure. But that was impossible if she wanted to continue with the work she was doing. And she did. Both for her own very selfish reasons and for the more noble goal of helping her country. She was somewhat ashamed to admit that it was the former that drove her far more than the latter. First for Allie, then for her brother, Max, who had been spirited away somewhere to protect both him and the DEA agent he'd been asked to protect.

For her it was about family and minimizing the danger to them. The Ghost was a threat to her country and Fuentes was a threat to her brother, Max, whom the drug lord wanted dead because of Max and Rio's humiliating escape from Fuentes's compound. That terrible double threat had to be eliminated.

But Jammer's recent confessions rattled her. He obviously had feelings for her. He'd orchestrated Miyagi's death so that she would be safe—at great personal danger to himself and his boss. She wasn't really sure what that said about him or his motivations, but she couldn't exactly come out and ask him. Besides, she didn't really want to know. It would only make matters worse.

Especially since she was unable to find that place inside her that would let her lie to herself, or at least come up with some small thing—anything, really—that she could latch on to as a means of protecting herself. Because the truth of the matter was that she wanted everything he did.

He'd never been far from her waking thoughts, despite the elapsed time since their last meeting, and no promise of ever seeing each other again. And damn, but he'd consumed her dreams for far, far too many nights.

But still, she'd never allowed herself the fantasy of this. Of them seeing each other again and reaching out for more than one another's willing and quite ready body.

What he wanted was dangerous bordering on terrifying, and she discovered she was ill prepared to deal with any part of it. She had a job to do. An important one. People were counting on her to deliver as she always did. This was not the time for selfish pursuits, much less delusional ideas that there could ever be something other than a very intense, deeply passionate and fulfilling physical relationship. Hell, she didn't even think she could handle *that* and keep her head on straight, which was why she'd tried to stay light and teasing.

There was no way she could tell him anything. His loyalty was to the Ghost and hers to Watchdog. She would see him and his boss in handcuffs, facing federal charges, before all was said and done.

"Jammer, we both know that I'm going to do what I have to do and so will you. So let's take the fun we have together while we can and enjoy it."

"I agree, but—" he cupped her chin "—if things

were different…" His tone was quiet, even sincere, if not particularly warm.

"It would require a different set of answers."

His mouth came down on hers unexpectedly, full of want and desire, like a rushing wave she couldn't hope to stop. It took her over completely, tossing her around until she was breathless and disoriented.

He broke the kiss and pressed his forehead to hers. "Get some rest and we'll talk later."

Not able to speak, she nodded and he turned to go. But before he left the room, she heard his voice, thick with emotion. "Just one question."

"Jammer, don't."

"I have to know, Gina. If there was a chance for us, would you take it?"

She had to struggle to find her sense of balance, since every facet of her equilibrium was threatened, physically, emotionally, intellectually.

"I wish it was that simple," she said, not able to commit to anything and keep her sanity.

He accepted her answer and left her standing there with her back against the wall, as if it was the only thing that held her upright.

WHAT THE HELL WAS WRONG with him? Not the smartest move he'd ever made. She had said she understood the score, but she was dead wrong. She didn't know jack. He was balanced on a fine wire here. A balance he desperately needed to maintain, since if he fell either way it would spell disaster.

Yet all of a sudden, everything he'd planned was

inconsequential to this woman and her welfare. Everything he'd promised, vowed, and every deal he'd ever made.

He wanted—needed—to create more distance. Mentally, anyway. He wasn't used to his thoughts being so clouded, and he knew his judgment would be off because of it. He simply had to find an edge and hold on to it for both their sakes.

There was too much at risk for each of them.

She was playing a lethal game and she didn't have all the cards. He did. And ultimately, he would have to be the one who won.

His cell rang and he pulled it out. "Yeah."

"How are things progressing?"

"There are some complications, but I'm dealing with them." The whole thing could blow up in Jammer's face if he wasn't careful, but he'd never reveal that to the man at the other end of the line.

"The woman?"

Jammer started to pace in agitation. He never lost it, but he didn't like Gina being scrutinized. "No, she's actually providing the solutions, but we both know how that came about."

"Yes, we're both aware of how resourceful her contacts can be.… We're agreed that you will use her, then neutralize her."

Jammer felt immediate resistance, and his throat knotted up. He had agreed. But that was before. Before he'd experienced what it was like to touch her, hold her, be deep inside her. That was before he knew her. Things

had changed, and the game pivoted on a very dangerous fulcrum.

"I don't like the sound of that silence. We agreed."

"I know," Jammer said.

"Don't let your johnson make the decisions for you.
You need to remember the name Shane McMasters
along with the names of the others who died. They gave
their lives for the cause."

"Listen, don't lecture me," Jammer growled. "She's
been a valuable resource in all this. Fuentes has to go
down, that's what we both believe. You let me decide
how that was going to happen. There is no one on this
planet who wants him out of the picture more than I do.
So honor *your* damn agreement and let me do this my
way."

"I'm just pointing out important facts."

"Like what?"

"Like you've lost your perspective. That fiasco with
DEA Agent Marshall was foolish. You risked exposure,
and if Fuentes had figured out it was you who contacted
Max Carpenter and spilled Rio's location, we would
have failed the mission."

Jammer's heart clenched in his chest and then released. Rio was safe. "It worked out for both our benefits. She and that FBI guy are now off our backs. And
Fuentes is now focused on what he has to do. So we don't
need to rehash that. I wasn't going to stand by and let
her die. I couldn't."

"No, I understand that. But it was a risk, just like the
woman is a risk."

He thought of her then, that soft, sassy mouth, silky-smooth skin and his need to hear her voice and see her smile. "A calculated one. The closer she is to me, the better I can keep an eye on her." And the easier it was for him to touch her, take that soft, sassy mouth and make her cry out his name.

"Keep me apprised, and watch your back."

"I will."

Jammer closed the phone with an audible snap. It had been a reality check. So much had been sacrificed. He would do what his partner suggested. Use Gina, then neutralize her. That was the way it had to be.

A ghost was insubstantial and so, unfortunately, were his dreams.

4

CALLIE CLOSED HER EYES when he left the room, knowing she was on the verge of something so darkly forbidden that if she gave in to it she wouldn't ever be the same. Even now, she sensed that once this op was over, she would be changed, and there wasn't one thing she could do about it.

Damn her need for justice.

Damn her need for Jammer.

She stopped on the landing and peeked out the window. Jammer was walking with Jim to a small wooden shed, and they disappeared inside. She dashed down the rest of the stairs, listening for any telltale sounds of someone still in the house. Nothing and no one.

She went into the study and closed the door. Making her way over to his desk, she quickly riffled through it, but found nothing that would indicate he'd had any contact with the Ghost, or who the man was. She then focused on the laptop. She was not savvy enough with computers to break into it in the short time she had, so she pulled out her cell and dialed Damian Frost, Watchdog's resident computer geek.

He answered on the first ring. "Took you long enough, love."

"Don't give me a hard time or I'll kick your Irish ass."

Many people when they first met Damian gave him a wide berth, for he exuded a lethal and deadly quality. But Callie was used to walking right into the tiger's den and pretending she belonged there. It was second nature to her.

He laughed and said, "What's the IP address?"

Callie read it to him, and while he was working his geeky magic, she went to the door to make sure Jammer wouldn't catch her unawares.

Her heart squeezed in her chest thinking about what she would have to ultimately do. The look in Jammer's eyes when she arrested him and turned him over to the courts would haunt her for the rest of her life.

Suddenly, she wanted to run, to get away from the reality of her mission. She turned back to his computer, thinking she could yank it from the desk, shut it off and tell Damian that Jammer had returned. She even took a step in that direction.

But caught herself. That would be treason and she'd sworn an oath. She couldn't let feelings for a man stand in her way. No matter how much her stomach knotted and her heart twisted in her chest.

"What are you doing in here?"

Adrenaline pumped hard into her system and she whirled at the sound of his deep, demanding voice. She met his gaze—sharp and intense as it always was, but now there was a hint of suspicion.

"You startled me," she murmured, forcing a smile. "I couldn't sleep, so I came down to see if I could pass the time with a book."

"A book?" he said, his eyebrows cocking, his mouth firming.

"Yes, a book. Are you insinuating that I wouldn't get pleasure from reading?"

His eyes flamed at the word *pleasure,* but Callie couldn't allow that to sidetrack her.

Hopefully, Damian had finished what he needed to do. Jammer went to the computer and looked at it, then at her. Callie's attention was on his library. She was pretending to peruse the books, but when her eyes snagged on Scottish poetry, she reached up and pulled the volume from between two leather-bound books.

"Scottish poetry?" She turned toward him, but Jammer was looking at the laptop with interest. Finally, he powered it down and closed the cover.

"What?" he said, as if whatever he had found on the computer had distracted him. She edged toward the door just in case he had discovered what she had been doing in his library. But she froze when he stared up at her.

"What did you say?"

She held up the text. "Scottish poetry. You are Scottish, aren't you?"

"I'd like people to think so," he said.

"Is something wrong?"

"No. Why? Should there be something wrong?"

She smiled and opened the volume in her hand as

if she didn't have a care in the world. Even her heart remained calm, beating normally. Written on the page in a neat hand was an inscription. "To my son. Here is a bit of our heritage. Although we're Americans, it'll help you understand your roots and where you came from."

The words touched her—a father giving a collection of poetry to his son so that he could have a sense of family and belonging.

Moments later she felt his hand on her nape, the warmth sending little prickles of sensation down her back and arms, but she kept her eyes glued to the page. "Did you read this?" she asked.

"Do you want me to tell you it's all for show?"

She closed the book, wishing he didn't evade every question she asked him. It was like *he* was the one who was the ghost.

"We have to be on our guard all the time. It's the nature of the business. So you don't have to tell me anything you don't want to tell me. We aren't a couple. We don't have any intention of staying together. I know this is a deal with fringe benefits. So you can lie to me if you wish and I'll pretend that it's the truth."

"Then why do you ask me so many questions?"

Callie's stomach jumped. Of course, the reason was because she was undercover to reveal the identity of the Ghost, and how to get to him. But if she was honest with herself, the *real* reason was because she wanted to know. She had this insatiable need to discover everything about Jammer.

But she tamped all of that down and responded with

the easiest answer. "Just wondering. You're an enigma, Jammer. Just trying to find out what's behind it."

"You'd be better off not knowing anything, Gina."

"You're probably right." He was, too; she had to get her wits back. She had to keep telling herself that this man wasn't who he seemed to be. He was in a dangerous business. He bought and sold weapons to perpetuate wars and death. He did it for profit. She couldn't be blinded by the way he treated her or how she felt when she was close to him.

Just because she couldn't reconcile what he'd done for her sister or the DEA agent didn't change the cold, hard facts. Jammer, the Ghost and—if she could manage it—Fuentes would all go down and be nothing but names on a prison roster when she was done.

She closed the book and went to return it to the shelf, working to corral her feelings, to get the right perspective on the situation.

But he bent his head down, his lips close to her ear. "What if I said that my ancestry *is* Scottish? That the book you hold was a present from my father, who wanted me to understand my lineage? Who thought that it was important to know where you came from before you found out where you were going? Who every day of his life gave me the wisdom and the nurturing that a father is supposed to give his son? What if I told you that he instilled in me a sense of place, an anchor to ground me? An anchor that has helped me in both hard times and good times?"

She steeled herself against the tortured tone of his voice, the raw emotion in his hands as they settled on her shoulders and squeezed gently. The trouble with being undercover was that she had to decipher what was real and what was fabricated. She had to step lightly to keep herself alive, and not fall for a charming gunrunner with a depth she hadn't expected and couldn't buy into. Her heart had to remain untouched.

She turned around and faced him. "I would say that you're very good at lying, Jammer." She tried to push down the lump in her throat as she pushed the book into his hands.

"I would have to be lying, wouldn't I? With a father like that, with that kind of upbringing—to be that boy, one lucky enough to have that kind of parenting—I wouldn't have turned out like me. A ruthless, greedy bastard, selling death."

She smiled as if it was the most natural thing in the world. "Exactly. You ought to think about writing fiction. You'd be very good at it."

"No, the thoughts I have in my head should stay there. Truth is more chilling than fiction. Keeping you alive will be enough for me to worry about."

"Why is that?"

"I've lost everyone who matters to me. I've got enough death on my conscience to last me more than one lifetime."

A thick, heavy silence hung in the air as their gazes held. Jammer's expression was turbulent, wistful, his fingers tight on her upper arms. She had the realization that he could have snapped her in half like a twig. She had never been quite so aware of the differences in their sizes, had never felt quite so overwhelmed by a man before.

"I've got enough death on my conscience to last me…" The words sank into her brain one by one to be scrutinized and a chill ran through her.

She stared at him for a long moment, watching him struggle to rein back the emotions that swirled in his eyes. She forced herself to relax by degrees, and breathed easier as his grip loosened. His hands settled on her shoulders.

"Would you like to unburden yourself?" she asked softly.

Very deliberately he lifted his hands from her shoulders and turned away from her. "No, I wouldn't."

She couldn't admit she was shaken or show that her legs and her heart had been affected by his words. She wouldn't believe that the affection in his voice, that terrible sense of loss in his eyes, was real. She was the one in charge of the situation. She was the one who had to remain calm and aloof.

She walked out of the room, digging in her pocket for her cell phone. She had a new determination to call Damian and find out if he'd gotten what he needed, or if she would have to make another trip down here to fulfill her mission.

"I think I will take that nap now, Jammer. Wake me in about an hour, would you?"

She vowed not to let the image of him standing there holding that book in his hands affect her as she headed for the stairs, her fingers already pressing the digits as she climbed. The faster she found out who the Ghost was, the faster she could get out of this situation.

She stopped on the steps and closed her eyes. Damn him and his secrets and his feigned vulnerability. For that was what it was. He was good, but she would have to be better.

She ignored the voice in her head that told her she was wrong. She wasn't wrong.

When Damian answered, she stepped into Jammer's room and closed the door.

JAMMER STOOD IN THE library, the leather of the book smooth against his palms. Why did she have to choose this volume over all the others? It was the only one in the room that was connected to a dead man. A ghost.

He felt all the ghosts in his life crowding him. Shifting his shoulders at the deep well of pain and loss, he reached up and slid the book back in place.

She was killing him by slow degrees. For the first time he chafed at the constraints he'd agreed to willingly when he went into this arrangement.

She was far too close, and every facet of his equilibrium was threatened, physically, emotionally, intellectually.

The urge to tell her the truth was there, the words right on the tip of his tongue. And that urge was so strong it actually made his insides cramp. He knew she couldn't possibly guess at what was really going on.

He was disappointed that she hadn't questioned him further, tried to glean whether or not his little "story" about his father was real.

His brain scrambled to logically weigh all the pros and cons of truly opening up to her, but his head was in a constant war with the reactions of his body and his heart. It was all such a huge jumble, there was no way he could make a rational judgment. Not with her looking at him with those bright and direct eyes and him wanting all sorts of things that were in conflict with why he was here and what he'd promised to get done. But his mind wouldn't stop spinning, teasing him with ridiculous possibilities, ones that should seem outrageous at best, terrifying at worst. And yet he couldn't stop that little voice from whispering tauntingly, teasingly, that perhaps it was possible he could somehow come out of this alive and free, and she might be the one woman with whom he could become whole.

Yeah, he was very good at spinning fiction—both with his words and in his head.

WHEN CALLIE WOKE UP the sun was low in the sky and she felt refreshed. She took a quick shower, then put on a pair of tight black shorts and a skimpy white cotton peasant top that bared her midriff.

Slipping her feet into a pair of black gladiator sandals, she exited the room, listening intently for any noise from the interior of the house. Hearing nothing, she walked downstairs and out into the yard. Wondering if Jammer had gone back to the shed, she made her way there. Pulling open the door, she was greeted with the sight of him dressed in a pair of cutoff denim shorts and a muscle T-shirt, standing next to a wooden table.

The aroma of alcohol laced with…cherries hit her as she stepped inside and shut the door.

"What are you doing?"

He looked around, his hair spiky, his eyes a bit lazy. He smiled and it was as if the sun came out in that small space. His teeth were white in the dimness and she literally had to catch her breath.

"Tasting the cherries to see if the brandy is ready."

"I'd say you've done your fair share of tasting."

He laughed. "I have. Come over here and help me."

"You were supposed to wake me."

"I know, but you were tired and I thought I'd do some more work before you got up."

"This is work?" she asked with an arched brow.

"It is." He laughed again and she realized he was a bit tipsy.

And she had to wonder if he'd come out here to escape from the tortured thoughts that haunted him.

"I've lost everyone who matters to me."

"I've got enough death on my conscience to last me…"

Who had he lost? Who had he cared about? Why were their deaths on his conscience?

She stopped herself from going down that road. It was dangerous to want that knowledge. She had all she could handle just getting through this op.

"Come here," he said softly. Something in his voice sent off fireworks in her midriff. At least she could pretend that was part of the op.

She approached him and could immediately feel the heat from his body as she got closer.

"I don't want to interrupt your...work," she said with a teasing smile.

"Tasting cherries is one of my favorite things to do. I don't mind sharing," he said. His eyes ran down her body to her groin, where they lingered, frank and outrageous.

She didn't move. Couldn't move with the aura of sin around him like a halo. He was temptation personified.

She had the sense, as she looked up into that calm, stunningly handsome face, that he was running possible scenarios through his head. Hot, dark, erotic. The air around them seemed suddenly charged with his powerful sexuality. It enveloped her, penetrating through the pores of her skin and stoking her blood with fire.

A delicate shiver of arousal rippled through her, followed closely with an aching tension deep in her core.

She couldn't help remembering the way his words about his father had touched her even though she hadn't wanted them to.

Sympathy was equated with weakness in her line of business; it could draw a person into a situation where perspectives could become warped, and emotions took over where logic should rule. But she'd already succumbed to it once.

He startled her with his next words.

"You don't trust me," he whispered, tenderly brushing the wet strands of her short hair then grazing his fingertips along the line of her cheekbone. "You shouldn't. I'm not good for you."

The warning was diluted to nothing by the sadness

in his face. His mouth twisted into a half smile that was cynical and weary. His dark eyes looked a hundred years old. Bad Jammer. The devil in cutoff denim. Self-professed seducer. Warning her away. He didn't see the paradox, but Callie did. He was nobody's hero, but he would save her from himself.

She had spent too much of her life with truly evil people. Jammer claimed to be bad and she had the reports to prove it. But why didn't she sense it in him? She wouldn't want him to kiss her right now, touch her, hold her while the scent of desire and cherries surrounded her.

He's deliciously dangerous.

Yes, she had thought that. And if Jammer himself wasn't dangerous, then what she felt for him when he was this near surely was. She couldn't fall for him, not for his body or his tarnished soul or his allure of the forbidden. There was no room in her life for a rogue. She couldn't have her heart stolen by a man like him. She was above that. She had to be.

She told herself that. But then he touched her, setting off a fire in her blood.

He gripped her waist, pulling her close, his hands warm and firm on her bare skin.

"This isn't what I ever intended," he said, lowering his head, his gaze on her mouth.

"Yeah, I know. Me, either."

He laid his mouth gently on hers, his kiss soft, but only for a moment, like testing the waters. Then it blossomed, and he kissed her as if the world was coming to an end, rolling his mouth over hers, his hands molding her to him like a second skin.

His kiss stole her breath away.

Her head was swimming and her body came alive. Damn, he was good at this. She wanted it to go on— would have in that second risked her life to stay right here and let him take her like some trophy.

But to her surprise, he broke the kiss and stepped back. "Got to get this job done. Want to help?"

Regaining some of her equilibrium, she braced her hand on the smooth wooden workbench behind her. "Yes, if it'll get it done any faster."

He chuckled. "Patience is a virtue."

"Patience sucks."

"Exactly what I would expect you to say, Gina."

She shrugged without apology.

He opened a jar and poured the reddish-black contents into a colander, straining it into a bowl beneath. The smell of the cherries filled Callie's nose. The fruit remaining in the colander was soft from the fermenting.

Jammer picked up a spoon and selected a cherry. "Don't take it whole. Lick it first...." His lean jaw clenched, as if he was barely holding on to his restraint.

Fire licked through her, deep and low.

He smelled sweet and tasted tart, and she thought she'd rather eat him than the cherry he held out to her on the tip of the spoon.

She indulged him because he was making her wait. Callie put out her tongue and licked at the cherry on the spoon, allowing her mouth to absorb the hot, spicy richness. "Oh God, that's amazing."

His gaze darkened with heat. "Now, bite it in half."

He watched raptly as she did so, her lips tingling from the juices. She closed her eyes as the liqueur's flavor burst on her tongue. When she swallowed, the brandy burned a path down her throat to settle in her empty stomach like a bomb, radiating heat outward like the concussion from an explosion.

She heard him exhale a deep breath and she smiled before she opened her eyes. Giving him an even badder bad-girl smile that told him she loved having the upper hand, she leaned forward and tried to take the half of the cherry still on the spoon.

He pulled it away and shook his head. He set the spoon down, grasped her around the waist and lifted her easily up onto the table. Spreading her thighs apart, he settled in between them, bracing his hands on either side of her hips.

"Are we done tasting?" she asked with a pout.

The feel of his lips on hers was exquisite, warm and heated, undeniably demanding. When their tongues touched, then tangled silkily, sparks ignited inside her stomach. He tasted like wild, untamed lust, and she thrilled at the amazing sense of feminine power that she could make this man so hungry for her.

With a low growl deep in his throat, he closed the scant distance between them and pressed his lean body up against hers, his strong thighs on either side of hers, trapping her so his thick, impressive erection made itself known. She could feel the heat and hardness of his chest crushing her breasts and the breathtaking ripple of muscle in his belly and flanks as he shifted even closer.

Lost in the need for him, Callie reveled in the unadulterated passion exploding between them—without thoughts of the rules of the game they were playing, or her "job" getting in the way of her pleasure. Letting instinct take over, she slid her hands around to his jean-clad bottom, molded her palms to his firm buttocks and arched into him.

The effect was like a lightning strike, and he slanted his mouth over hers for a deeper kiss, a hotter, wetter possession. His hand stole beneath her top, and she shivered as his fingers skimmed their way upward, and then curled around the plump curve of her breast. Her bra was lacy and sheer, the fabric thin and insubstantial, and she was eternally grateful that there was no excess padding to separate the fire of his touch from her aching flesh. Then he found her nipple and rolled the taut, throbbing tip between his thumb and forefinger, and she nearly came undone right then and there.

As if sensing just how fast their encounter was spiraling out of control, he slowed their kisses, leaving her feeling flushed, and both of them breathing fast. As she tried to calm her erratic heartbeat, he licked the inside of her mouth, gently bit on her lower lip and soothed the slight sting with the soft, damp stroke of his tongue.

Eyes closed, she let her head fall back, exposing the column of her neck. With his hand still on her breast, he dipped his head, his silky-soft hair brushing her jaw as he suckled on a patch of skin, then nibbled his way up to her ear. She inhaled a sharp breath and another surge of sensation swamped her as she drew in the warm, masculine scent that was uniquely his own.

Damn, he smelled delicious. She wanted to take a big bite of him and lick his burning, salty skin, feel the heat and steel of him against her lips, taste him with her tongue....

She groaned and reached out to snag the T-shirt he was wearing. Pulling up, she ripped it off his body so that she could settle her hands against all that taut muscle.

His skin was like velvet as she ran her palms over the planes of his chest, brushing over his flat nipples and down the sides of his torso to the heavy muscle of his back.

"What about the cherries, the bottling?" she asked.

"We'll finish up, don't worry," he responded. "Later."

5

"I'D RATHER FOCUS on the fruit of your body right now."

Jammer couldn't get enough of Gina, her blue eyes wide with the same anticipation he felt thrumming through his veins. Her eagerness fueled his and he loved watching her come.

He'd have to absorb as much as he could of their time together, for too soon it would come to an end.

Once he screwed over Fuentes, the drug lord wouldn't soon forgive or forget who had taken him down. Even from prison, Fuentes would wield the power to kill Jammer and anyone involved with him.

He would need to disappear and assume another identity, and he couldn't take the risk of dragging Gina into that scenario. Not when he'd been responsible for so many bodies already. He couldn't bear having her death on his conscience, as well.

But he wouldn't think about that now. Now was the time to make some memories that would last him a lifetime.

The scent of her mingled with the aroma of fermented cherries like an aphrodisiac, rich and thick with sensual promise, tantalizing and seducing him even further.

As he'd demonstrated before, he wasn't one to rush a good thing...especially when it came to sex. He liked to savor the seduction, enjoy the slow, arousing buildup of hot I-have-to-have-you-now kind of foreplay, make all the spine-tingling sexual tension last, so when they finally came together there would be no forgetting what sex with him was like.

"Hmm, on second thought..." He flashed her a wicked grin as an idea formed in his mind. "Maybe we can do both at the same time."

"Oooh, I like the sound of that," she said, her eyes flickering with interest and excitement.

He skimmed his fingers along the curve of her waist and watched as her nipples peaked against her top. Her natural response to his touch caused his own body to tighten in places, too. "Are you feeling daring and adventurous?"

She laughed breathlessly. "Absolutely. Bring it on."

"You ever done body shots?"

"No, but I know what they are. What did you have in mind?"

"Why don't we play it by ear," he said, his lips dipping to hers again. Burying his hands in her hair, he moved his mouth over hers, slow and languid, his teeth nipping at her plump bottom lip. Then he slid his tongue inside, and she met every hot, moist sweep of his tongue with her own. She tasted like spice and sweet cherries as fine and appetizing as the brandy.

He used his mouth to seduce and tease. Pulling away, he kept his lips just out of reach of hers, taunting her. But Gina wasn't a passive woman. She caught him behind his nape and pulled his mouth back to hers.

He laughed softly against her lips, accepting that he would never forget this woman. The thought of being without her made him press his mouth harder, the need inside driving him.

He lifted her and eased her against his groin. The heat between them flared and they both groaned.

He trailed his fingers up her quivering thighs to the crux of her sex, where he could feel the dampness, and he guessed she wasn't wearing panties under her tight, hip-hugging shorts. He smoothed his palms over the curve of her buttocks, then leaned over her, holding her heavy-lidded gaze as he pulled the white peasant top off her in one smooth stroke, baring her upper body to his hungry gaze.

He brushed his fingers over the swells of her breasts, and her breathing deepened in anticipation as he dragged the stretchy, sheer cups of her bra down, releasing those two full, perfectly shaped mounds of flesh. Her nipples puckered, tightening into hard beads that looked as delicious as two cherries.

She curled her hand around the nape of his neck and drew his head downward. "Put your mouth on me," she urged huskily. "Please."

He pulled back slightly as she thrust her body toward him. Reaching into the colander, he grabbed a few cherries and crushed them, releasing the juices locked inside.

Then he smeared his fingers over each of her nipples and heard her suck in a breath.

He gently grazed a nipple with his teeth and another gasp escaped her. The taste of hot woman and sweet cherries burst on his tongue when he laved her searing, juicy breasts.

"Mmm," he murmured. "Sugar and spice and everything nice."

And finally, a long-drawn-out moan sounded when he took her deep into his mouth and suckled hungrily on her soft flesh, cleaning up as much of the juice and crushed cherries as he could.

Her fingers raked through his hair as he gave the other breast equal attention, until she was writhing beneath him and panting in that needy way he recognized all too well. He blazed fiery, moist kisses up to her throat and along her jaw as he moved over her and settled his hips against hers. He pressed his solid erection— still confined behind the fly of his cutoffs—against the crotch of her shorts, exactly where he knew she'd need that firm, driving pressure the most.

He watched her eyes darken with desire, and could feel the heat and dampness of her through the heavy denim. Jammer did his best to keep his focus on her and away from the demanding ache in his cock.

Lowering his head, he kissed her, while moving against her in a slow, sensual motion that was as intimate as the act of sex itself.

Her hands caressed and kneaded his shoulders. She glided her palms over his taut belly and around to his back, where she kneaded her fingers into the muscles in an attempt to urge him to a faster tempo. Wrapping her legs around his thighs, she grabbed his ass so she could control the depth and pace of his strokes.

He wrenched his mouth from hers and managed a laugh. "Damn, maybe patience is overrated."

"Exactly," she said, her breathing hard and rasping.

"You'll have to find a little bit more patience, sweetheart," he said as he curled his arm around her waist, lifted her and stripped the tight shorts off her body. He also removed the lacy bra, so that she was completely naked on the wooden table.

"No fair. You're still dressed."

"Don't worry about that right now," he said softly. With his palm on her chest he leaned her back until she was resting against the wall. Then he grasped her just under the knees and pushed her legs apart until she was bared to him.

"Oh damn, Jammer. I want you."

"Soon. Very soon, baby."

He grabbed more cherries and crushed them, then rubbed his fingers over her clit. Gina cried out, but he didn't give her a moment to catch her breath. His mouth captured her clit with suctioning pulls and swirls of his tongue, and she came with quick thrusts of her hips.

His restraint finally broken, Jammer undid his cutoffs and let them and his briefs drop to the floor.

When he moved back to the table, she was waiting. Her hand snaked out, captured his throbbing cock and guided him to her. He needed no encouragement as he slipped inside her, the juice from the cherries sliding along his shaft with a tingling, sensual burn.

The heat of her sex scorched him. Made him move with deep, slow thrusts inside her.

Then she tensed and quickened, captivated as she reached between them to feel him glide wetly into her, then retreat. Her touch was heavy and bold, and he loved this side of her. Most of the time she was out there for everyone to see, but this Gina, this intimate Gina, was all his.

Jammer wanted more, to connect when he hadn't—wouldn't—allow himself to have anything beyond casual and quick sex. Playing it safe had become ingrained in him for three long years. Then she'd opened that door in Paris and he would never be the same. Casual and Gina just didn't mesh.

But he and Gina did.

In a profound and primal way that he hadn't thought possible.

He knew that every moment he spent with her would only make it that much harder to separate when the time came. His chest and throat constricted at the thought, so he pushed it aside and focused on the incredible sensations she was generating with her sleek, sexy body.

"Jammer, please," she begged softly.

His control severed and his hips plunged faster into the tight core of her. She wrapped her legs around him, squeezing hard and holding on to him as if she would never let go.

He deepened his thrusts, his possession raw and savage. Matching his rhythm, she finally came, holding nothing back and whispering her satisfaction. One more flex of thick muscle and his own climax roared over him, joining hers. And she felt it, accepted the power of him, the brutal honesty of the moment.

Jammer threw his head back, caught, the wild grip of her flesh wringing him. Splintered rapture shredded his composure. Yet in the throes of release, he was aware of her smooth skin, the scent that was quintessentially Gina, the soft gasp as she absorbed the pleasure he was giving her. "Damn, Gina," he murmured, slipping his arms around her, the last threads of passion dissolving under a slow, thick kiss.

Seconds passed as they held each other. Darkness had fallen outside the window and the rumble of Gina's stomach broke the silence.

He chuckled and let her go. "Sounds like you need some food."

"I'm starving. Those cherries made me a little tipsy on an empty stomach."

"Let's quickly finish this bottling and we'll head into the house. I'll make you a meal."

She looked at him with one eyebrow cocked. "Oh my God, don't tell me you cook."

"I do."

"If you also iron, I'm going to keep you."

He laughed and felt that same constriction in his chest. He told himself it wasn't possible. He dressed quickly, handing Gina her clothes, then made quick work of bottling the brandy, stoppering it and setting it on a shelf with the others to receive the special Craving Brandy label.

Holding hands, they left the shed and walked to the

house. Gina stopped suddenly and said, "Wow, check out the stars. The night sky is gorgeous."

Jammer looked up and took in the beauty of the smudged blue sky dotted with lights. She was right.

"Let's eat outside. It's so pretty," she exclaimed.

"No problem. There's a patio by the kitchen door that overlooks the pool and the vineyards."

"Sounds simply wonderful."

They entered the house and headed upstairs, where they took a quick shower that soon got out of hand. Once again Gina's stomach rumbling sent them back on course. Sitting at the island, she flipped open her cell phone. "Let me make some calls and see if I can put something together while you cook."

He nodded and went to the fridge, pulling out what he needed. He set water to boil and when it was ready added lasagna noodles.

He started off with olive oil in a pan, followed by onions, mushrooms, garlic, basil, chicken broth and cornstarch. Once it was simmering, he added cream cheese, stirring slowly as it melted, releasing mouth-watering aromas.

"That smells heavenly. Is it going to be ready soon?"

"Nope. Got to layer it together and put it in the oven. You're going to have to pull that patience out again."

"Well, hurry it up."

Jammer added sour cream, artichokes and crab meat into the pan, seasoning with salt and pepper. Next, he spread some of the mixture along each lasagna noodle, rolled it up and set it in a shallow casserole. When the dish was full, he covered it with foil and popped it into the oven, setting the timer.

"Let's go outside until it's done. Enjoy the night," he said as he opened the French doors and stepped out. The patio was tiered, gently sloping down to a sparkling turquoise pool. He walked to the second tier and settled into a chaise longue and pulled Gina into his lap. She curled against him, snuggling her head under his chin.

"So where did you learn to cook?" she asked.

"My mother taught me." He lifted a hand and stroked it over her hair. His heart constricted at the thought of his mother.

"Oh," Gina said, a cautious tone to her voice.

She knew as well as he that they were getting into personal territory, and he wasn't sure that they should.

"Are they still alive?"

"No, they aren't. It's better that they're not," he said, then regretted the words.

"Because of what you do for a living?"

He shrugged, as if it was unimportant, when it was far from that. "Yeah," he answered, but that wasn't the truth at all. It had to do with the pain and agony they would have had to endure, knowing they had lost their only son. He wouldn't have been able to participate in this plan to take down Fuentes if they had lived.

"Any luck with your contacts?" he asked, effectively changing the painful subject.

"Yes, I think so. I'm waiting for a couple of calls. A guy in Rome who I think will have some of what you need—namely the surface-to-air missiles—and I have a guy in London who should be able to deliver on the other required items."

"Excellent. Fuentes will be calling tomorrow for an update on his order. It'd be good to be able to tell him we're moving forward."

"What is he like?"

"Fuentes? A freaking little girl in a grown man's body. When he doesn't get his way, he has these tantrums that are ridiculous to watch. How he ever built an empire is a mystery to me."

"Do you think there will be a possibility of more deals once you've supplied what he's asking for?"

Not if Jammer had any say in the matter. But he had a role to play here and he knew how to play it well. "Of course. Drug dealers always need weapons for the movement of their product. It's a fact of life."

"Will the Ghost be at the meeting with Fuentes?"

"Yes, he's going to make a rare appearance. Fuentes wants the transfer to happen in person. So my boss is committed." The Ghost would be there, all right, but Fuentes wasn't going to see it coming, and that gave Jammer great satisfaction.

"How about you let me go all the way on this deal? I'll make it worth your while."

"Gina, Fuentes is an animal and I don't trust him at all. I think it would be best if you stayed out of it."

"Jammer, come on. I could make some really good contacts and boost my business. You wouldn't deny me that, would you? Look at all the help I'm giving you. If it wasn't for me, you wouldn't have been able to fill Fuentes's order."

"That is true. I would have been royally fucked."

"Right, and not in a good way."

"Let me think about it."

"I'm not a fragile piece of glass, you know. I can take care of myself in this business. Miyagi caught me off guard, but it won't happen again."

Jammer cupped her face and met her blue eyes. "That threat has been neutralized. I made sure of it. I will do anything for you, Gina, but have a care when it comes to Fuentes. He's ruthless and heartless. He doesn't have any concern for human life. He takes it without impunity."

"Sounds like you have firsthand knowledge."

Jammer let her go and turned away. "I do, and that's not something I will discuss."

This time she took his face in her hands. "Did you lose people close to you at the hands of Fuentes?"

The guilt twisted like a knife inside him, and he squeezed his eyes shut against the pain. He tried to pull away but she wouldn't go. He sighed. "Don't ask me any more questions about Fuentes. It's time to check on dinner."

He felt her gaze on him, but ignored her, capturing her around the waist and setting her on her feet.

He could sense the tension in the air around him, snapping with electricity. When she touched his arm, he jolted as if he had received a shock.

"I'm very, very sorry."

"It was my fault," he whispered, the anguish almost palpable.

Without another word, she followed him into the house.

The smell in the kitchen made his mouth water. There were only five minutes left on the timer, so he grabbed two plates, trying to let what had happened outside slide off him as he'd done in the past. He wished she hadn't been there to witness his weak moment, but her sympathy had touched him in a place so deep he'd thought it was out of reach.

He placed rolls on each plate and quickly put together the ingredients for a salad.

When the timer went off he served the salad and then remembered the wine.

"Let me go down and get a bottle."

"In the dungeon?" she said in a comical stage whisper.

He chuckled. "Yes, want to come with me?"

"Oh, most definitely."

The stairs to the wine cellar were cut stone, as were the walls. At the bottom were rows and rows of wine, some of it his as well as other vintage bottles he'd picked up here and there.

In the corner sat an old fashioned rack. A mock Scottish castle had to have a dungeon and the requisite torture device, even if it was nothing but a prop.

"Oh no, this looks…dangerous."

"It's for show, but it's got restraints and it does work."

"Have you ever used it on your victims?"

He laughed. "No," he said, and slapped her on the ass. "But there's a first time for everything."

"Oooh, you could be the evil overlord and I'll be your

captured noblewoman who won't sell you the land you covet. You have to torture me to get me to submit."

"Hmm, that has potential. But I can think of better torture than stretching your joints until they feel like they're going to pull apart."

"I bet you can."

"Come on, let's get the wine. Our dinner's cooling and I'm starving."

Gina shot one more glance at the rack and followed him as he chose a white to compliment the crab.

Back upstairs, they went outside to enjoy their dinner. The conversation revolved around business and the ins and outs of gunrunning, including the many pitfalls of federal intervention.

When Gina went to pour more wine, the bottle was empty. They both went down to the cellar for another, but she got too close to Jammer at the bottom, brushing by him, inflaming him.

After her shower she had changed into a daisy-flowered miniskirt and a gauzy yellow top that showed a purple bra beneath.

Unable to help himself, he came up behind her and encircled her waist. Slipping his hands underneath the material, he said softly, in a perfect Scottish accent, "Milady, you will consent to sell me your land when I am through with you."

Gina laughed softly and gasped as his hands cupped her breasts.

"You canna make me do something against my will. I will defy you at every turn."

He kissed her neck, his mouth trailing up to the

delicate shell of her ear, where he whispered, "You will agree to that and more."

He started to undress her, and Gina pretended to fight him, turning to face him and pummeling his chest with her tiny fists. But he lifted her bodily and laid her on the rack, shackling her loosely.

Then he removed his clothing and walked over to get another bottle of wine, this time choosing champagne.

He returned to the rack and looked down at her. She might be the one constrained, but he was the one helpless. She was so fucking beautiful, exquisitely so, her agile, graceful body stretched out and completely under his power.

After trailing the neck of the bottle from her rapidly beating pulse point down to her high, firm breasts, he replaced the bottle with his own lips, quickly sucking each nipple into his mouth with a tug and a rake of his teeth, drawing a swift, hard gasp and an uncontrollable arch of her body.

"I want to sip you like this champagne."

"Use me to quench whatever thirst you have," she said, her gaze demanding he do his worst—or his best.

"I don't know if anything will quench my thirst for you," he admitted, and that would be true for the rest of his life—with or without her in it.

With the champagne still in his hand, he straddled her hips. Smiling with lascivious intent, he looked at the bottle, then down at her. "Let's see if we can put this to good use."

"Oh, if only you had the end of a mustache to twist, this would be perfect."

He laughed out loud.

He opened the champagne, the cork popping loudly in the room.

"A good sound. Should be nice and bubbly," she said.

He took a long pull of the clear, sweet wine, which got his taste buds tingling. Taking more into his mouth, he leaned down and kissed her, releasing the wine into her mouth for her to savor and swallow. He could taste the mingling of her luscious essence and the sweet nectar of the champagne, a heady aphrodisiac that made his whole body tense in sensual need. But he had other places to explore on her than her sumptuous lips.

He released her, but she wasn't quite ready to let him go. The restraints of the rack stopped her from reaching for him, however. "Jammer," she moaned feverishly.

"There are other things to taste," he said softly, tipping the bottle up until the golden liquid splashed onto one cherry-sweet nipple. It budded immediately into a hard, mouthwatering peak and Gina cried out. The chilled liquid against her hot skin produced another strangled moan when he splashed the other turgid bud. The wine ran in rivulets off the globes of her breasts, slid sensuously down the taut line of her stomach and pooled in her belly button.

She shuddered more from the sensation, he was sure, than the temperature of the wine. "You're getting me all wet!"

"Wet and wild for me."

"Oh, yes. Oh, hell yes!"

"It's great when a plan comes together." Laughing softly, he dipped his head and hovered over her wet and tantalizing breast, blowing a burning-hot breath against her sensitized nipple. She rolled her body in sensual abandon, her hands pulling at the restraints. "You teasing bastard."

She lifted her chest, straining for his mouth, and his cock tightened so hard he groaned. He'd never been this close to orgasm with a woman without her actually touching him.

Then he deliberately flicked his tongue across her nipple, the taste of her and the wine like a burst of electricity on his tongue. With an uncontrollable moan, he sucked her nipple into his mouth with a rough, strong pull. He worked it until she was writhing and thrashing, until every drop of the delectable wine was removed. Then he switched to her other one, taking her deep—deep enough that he could devour her.

Setting aside the bottle for a moment, he ran his tongue down to where her body cupped the wine. He lapped it up while he skimmed his fingers down her quivering belly to the top of her groin. Splaying his hands, he pushed her legs open to reveal to his hungry eyes the core of her sex. He ran his thumbs along her glistening folds, enjoying her intense moan and delectable shiver.

She was gloriously wet and about to get wetter.

He grabbed the bottle and ran the smooth glass neck along her mound and down to her hot pulsing center. She jerked in response. With deliberate slowness and care, he slipped the mouth of the bottle into her, then said huskily, "Arch for me."

When her hips moved, the champagne tipped and liquid rushed out, soaking her sex with the cool bubbly and sparkling froth.

His mouth clamped on to her and he tormented her with his tongue and mouth, licking, sucking at her sensitive flesh over and over again.

"Oh, damn," she moaned, and the automatic movement of her pelvis tipped the bottle once more. She gasped as more champagne poured out. Jammer caught the wine and her, drinking both in.

Her breath came in little puffs of pleasure, her body writhing beneath his ministrations as her orgasm rushed toward her. He could feel it crest and beat against his mouth as the champagne splashed with her frantic movements. His body aching for her, he glided two fingers inside her, at the same time sucking her clit hard, then laving her with his tongue. She pulsed against his mouth, her hips jerking and arching as she cried out, her body bowing up from the rack and tugging at the restraints as her climax exploded.

Captured by the sheer beauty of Gina's luminous pleasure, he let the almost-empty bottle go. His rock-hard cock throbbed in unison with her orgasm as he moved up her body and thrust into her as deeply as he could, the pleasure overtaking him, shredding his control. Her inner muscles contracted around him as he plunged into her without restraint.

He drove into her rough and fast, his pleasure building and tearing along his cock with blinding need. When his release burst over him, he lost everything that he was—his heart, his body and his soul—to her.

6

HOURS LATER, Callie woke up in Jammer's big bed, the memory of her time in the dungeon still tingling through her. The warm body tucked next to hers made her shift gently. It had been a while since she'd woken up next to a man. When it came to sex, she made sure it never occurred in her apartment. She needed the option to leave as soon as it became uncomfortable. Sort of a guy mentality, but closeness wasn't something she had allowed herself in the past years. She scooted back and didn't touch him, but let her gaze travel down his long body.

Jammer was a powerful man when clothed, exuding a charisma and confidence that made her knees weak. But with him fully naked, Callie saw that it wasn't the clothes that made the man.

She noticed a multitude of scars—a couple left by bullets. Her hands itched to touch him. But she had some work to do.

Quietly, she slipped from the bed, gathered her things and went into the bathroom. She showered quickly. After drying off, she tugged on a white, see-through mesh tank top and a pair of white lace boy-shorts underpants.

She went down to the kitchen to make a pot of coffee and phone Damian again away from Jammer's ears. The Irishman still hadn't found anything on Jammer's computer that could lead them to the Ghost, and he didn't think he would with further scrutiny, so she was back to plan A. She brought a carafe and cups up with her to the bedroom. Just as she was settling into the chaise longue in the corner of the bedroom to stare at Jammer's muscled-to-perfection body, her cell rang.

It was a contact she had in Belarus. He couldn't get her what she needed.

Afterward, she tapped on the keys and put the phone again to her ear. It was picked up after two rings. The deep British voice on the other end of the line was a bit slurred.

"Speak."

"Reggie, it's Gina."

"Hiya, love. You in London?"

"No, California."

"Ah, too bad. You need sumthin'?"

"Yes, I do, Reggie."

"Anythin' for you, love."

"I was hoping you'd say that. I need seven or eight hundred surface-to-air missiles, five thousand AK-47 rifles, three million rounds of ammunition, land mines, night-vision goggles, plus some ultralight planes that can be equipped with grenade launchers and missiles."

"Bugger me, that's a tall order."

"We needed them yesterday."

"We?"

"I'm working with the Ghost's guy, Jammer."

"I've heard of him. Well, I can maybe do half that. I can't get the missiles or the planes."

"I'll take it."

"Consider it done."

"We can be there by tomorrow." Callie looked at her watch. "Say 11:00 a.m. your time? The usual spot?"

"Yes, just you and him. Right?"

"Just the two of us."

"Tomorrow it is then, love. Cheerio."

As soon as she completed the call, her phone rang again. When she answered, it was her contact in Italy, Alberto Bianchi.

"*Ciao, bella.* I have heard that you wanted to speak with me."

"I do." Callie outlined what she was seeking, and Alberto said he could make up Reggie's shortfall. But he couldn't get his hands on the surface-to-air missiles or the planes, either.

"Do you know who can?" Callie asked.

When he named the person, Callie felt her stomach jump. The only arms dealer Callie would have avoided like the plague seemed to be the only one who could supply Jammer with what he needed on such short notice. The Italian told her that she'd have to see him tomorrow because he had a commitment. It forced Callie to call Reggie back to change their appointment to the end of the week.

She bit her lip, debating whether to dial the contact

that Alberto had named. She decided to wait and talk to Jammer about it before she made any firm plans.

Callie heard Jammer stir, and something shifted inside her when he reached for her in his sleep.

He woke with a start and instantly took in his surroundings. It seemed that the man was alert the moment he opened his eyes. When he saw her across the room, he sank into the pillows. Callie smiled from her vantage point near the French doors that opened onto a balcony. A soft morning breeze wafted through the room, caressing her bare shoulders and gently moving the white sheers near the doors.

"Good morning," she said, smiling. "Hungry? We have coffee." Reaching for the carafe, she poured him a cup.

"Why don't you bring that over here?" he said.

She rose with the cup in her hand, automatically adding the right amount of cream. Then she grabbed a blueberry muffin and the itinerary, and made her way over to the bed.

She sat down and offered him the cup and the muffin. He sat up and accepted the coffee, taking a sip. "Anything else come with this muffin?" His gray eyes twinkled.

She leaned down and smiled. "Tons of calories, but—" she patted his flat, washboard abs "—I think you can handle it."

He chuckled and bit off a chunk. "What else have you got there?"

"I've been busy," she said. "While you were sleeping,

I set up buys in Rome and London with a couple of my contacts."

"Who?"

"Alberto Bianchi and Reggie Smythe."

"Bianchi I've heard of, but Smythe…can't place him."

"Well, your reputation precedes you. I got the full order except for the surface-to-air missiles and the planes. I'm still working on those."

"Your contacts couldn't supply them, Gina?"

"Alberto and Reggie can't handle more than that. But it's a good start. We're better off than we were yesterday, and I haven't even scratched the surface of my contacts."

He nodded. "Okay, I trust you on this."

She knew he did, and those words cut into her deeper than any words from a man she intended to arrest ever could. He trusted her, much to his folly. She had him hooked, and she'd reel him in and then she would…walk away and prepare for the next mission.

That was her reality, not this sunlit room, in this gorgeous house nestled in the breathtaking landscape of Southern California, with this enticing, drop-dead-dangerous man.

But she never missed a beat or dropped out of her Gina cover. She played her part to the fullest extent. "Good, because Reggie and Alberto will deliver what they promised. If they don't, I'll make them sorry, and I won't need any help to do so."

Jammer took another sip of his coffee and polished off the muffin. "I'll help anyway."

A shiver ran down her spine at the menacing tone in his voice.

He rose and set the cup on the nightstand, disappearing into the bathroom. While he showered, Callie stepped out on the balcony and updated Gillian on her progress.

She ended the call just as Jammer exited the bathroom. He climbed into a pair of black boxer briefs and blue jeans.

"This gunrunner in London. Does he have blond hair and a Cockney accent?"

"Yes. I thought you didn't know him?"

"I don't, just heard about him."

He picked up the towel he'd dropped and vigorously rubbed his dark hair, leaving it in wet, tangled spikes.

"And?" she asked.

"Nothing bad that I remember. I just heard he has a thing for you."

"All men have a thing for me. I know how to handle those 'things' with a quick jab of my knee."

He laughed out loud. "Good. Then I won't have to kill him."

She eyed Jammer, trying to gauge whether he was serious or not. What she saw in his eyes sent another, more powerful shiver down her spine.

"Now, there's no need for jealousy or violence. That's never been a smart combination. I'm only interested in you, baby." She felt the truth of her words resonate against her heartstrings. Her hands itched to touch him.

"I still don't like it," he said, giving the full effect of a lethal Jammer.

"Awww, come on, sweetie. You're not going to make me regret getting you a firearm in London now, are you? The Brits don't really appreciate us crazy Americans acting like we're in the Wild West." She pouted and then smiled as that look faded from his eyes. And the urge to touch him ratcheted up a notch.

"Don't worry. You can be sure I'll be locked and loaded."

"Judging from my keen observation, baby, you don't need a gun for that."

Her gaze slid over him. The reality was far better than any fantasy she'd worked up during the few weeks they'd been separated. His heavy muscles stood out in stark relief as he picked up his cup and sipped his coffee, his eyes on her—not her body or anything else, but her face. It was intense; she felt it down to her bones. Her gaze slipped to his jeans. The top button was open. She wanted to peel those off and have her way with him. As if reading her mind, his mouth curved.

She reached out and smoothed her hands over his chest. "I'm really hating the airlines right now."

Jammer set the cup down. "I take it we don't have time because we've got a flight to catch?"

Her palms, hot from the warmth of his skin, tingled. The chemistry between them could cause a small fire— spontaneous combustion.

He bent down and she covered his mouth with a quick movement of her hand.

"Get packed," she told him, recognizing the look in his eyes. "Guns, deals."

"You're all business, aren't you?"

Smiling widely, she moved off the bed and squatted to grab her suitcase. "Get dressed, Jammer. Before I lose my business sense and peel you out of those jeans."

But she didn't get far. His warm hand slipped around her wrist and she found herself jerked up against him. His eyes locked to hers like a loaded gun. The experience of a fully aroused Jammer who wanted what he wanted was seductive, intimate and wholly unnerving.

"Jammer, the flight…"

Most of the time, she thought she had the tiger tamed, but at moments like this, when he exerted his formidable presence, Callie found that the taming was a complete and total illusion. What shocked her about him constantly was his ability to make her melt, when she knew in her brain that she shouldn't be doing anything of the sort. From the instant she'd met him, she'd lost that cool, controlled persona that had protected her from situations exactly like this.

She was playing a dangerous game, but she just couldn't seem to help herself. He made everything inside her come alive every second she was with him.

His mouth curved. "Who gives a fuck about the flight?"

Drawing a deep, measured breath to steady herself, she tilted her chin up and tried again. "We do. Remember Fuentes."

"That bastard can go to hell," he said. His tone dismissed the drug lord as if he was totally inconsequential. "Usually I prefer to take my time with you, Gina. Slow, long strokes that make you want to go crazy. But fast works for me, too."

He held her gaze, his eyes dark and intense, mesmerizing. "You're killing me with that outfit, and you expect me to keep my hands off you. You don't want me to, do you?"

Her breath hitched and she ran out of air, just like that. Her breasts pressed firmly to him, tingling from the provocative heat of his rock-solid chest. Her pulse tripped all over itself, and anticipation coiled tight and low in her belly.

"I want to suck your nipples right through that pure white mesh. Take those hard, hot peaks, the color of cherries, into my mouth and taste you."

"You are such a seductive bastard, but we don't have time…."

He leaned in, the clean, sharp smell of him making her lose her train of thought for a moment. Then it was totally lost when he said, "I bet you're hot and deliciously wet right now. I bet my cock would glide in like greased lightning."

She groaned and that was the end of his restraint. His mouth was scorching and demanding from the instant he assaulted hers, as if he was unleashing all the passion and hunger that he just couldn't contain. It spilled over in his almost savage kiss. He kissed her deeply, his mouth pressing harder until she tasted blood, and she wasn't sure if it was his or hers.

His hand fisted in her hair at her nape, while the other stroked down her spine and cupped her bottom and squeezed. Next thing she knew, she was flat on her back on the bed. Her senses reeled as he loomed over her, looking tough and sexy. She could feel the explosive energy coiling tighter and tighter inside his strong body.

His hands went to the thin straps of her top and dragged them down her arms until they caught in the crooks of her elbows and the mesh material bunched beneath her breasts. Without giving her time to breathe, he closed his blazing mouth over one firm nipple, then the other, using his tongue and teeth before sucking her hard and strong, and she cried out from the searing pleasure of it.

Her hips began to move against his, rubbing along his thickened erection, seeking relief from the growing, pulsing ache between her thighs. He swore and pulled his mouth from her breast, breathing heavily, his eyes electric.

"I need you inside, Jammer, inside."

His nostrils flared, and with a low, rumbling growl he stripped off his jeans and boxers, then her lacy panties. Before she could take another breath, he rose over her, fitting himself between her thighs. There was nothing gentle about the way he plunged into her and filled her to the hilt, nothing sweet about his deep, driving thrusts.

"Fuck, you're killing me," he said with agony.

Her body embraced every inch of him, met him stroke for stroke, matching his erotic rhythm as it sped out of control.

He groaned and tossed back his head, arching into her, surging higher, grinding harder, moving faster until she was gasping for breath and swept into a devastating climax.

Growling low in his throat, he surrendered to his own fierce orgasm. His hips pressed her farther into the bed, then farther still, nearly crushing her with the violent force of his release. His breath ragged, he collapsed on top of her and buried his face against her neck.

"Really," she said softly, against his brow. "Who gives a fuck about the flight?"

"I love it when you talk dirty," he mumbled into her throat, and they both erupted into laughter.

Callie was weak when it came to this one particular man, completely and utterly helpless to resist his allure, so unable to refuse him anything.

And that was going to cause her a wealth of heartache in the end.

DUE TO JAMMER'S *delay* they had to take a later flight, which put them into Rome's very busy Fiumicino Airport early in the morning. Finally, they got through security and customs, and were in a limo heading to their hotel—the St. George Roma, a quaint hotel Callie had never visited and Jammer had stayed in several times. It was decorated in a trendy style, with lots of travertine and marble on the walls and floors.

Callie was used to time changes, and jet lag had ceased to affect her. She was wide-awake and sleep wasn't an option, so Jammer suggested they go for a run before the heat and tourists took over the city.

Eager for the exercise, Callie changed into a T-shirt and shorts and followed Jammer out of their hotel.

It was still dark outside, but the streets were illuminated and easy to navigate. Dawn was about an hour away.

Jammer took her past St. Peter's Basilica and through winding streets as the city came awake. After thirty minutes of running they passed the Pantheon and, jogging in place, Callie stopped to take in the ancient structure.

It wasn't long before she could hear the sound of gushing water. It reached a crescendo when they emerged in a square and saw the Trevi Fountain, bathed in gold from the illumination of the lights.

Panting from their exertion, Jammer and Callie splashed themselves with the water from the fountain to cool off.

There were very few pedestrians around, but traffic was starting to increase in the area where three roads intersected, forming the square.

When their breathing had returned to normal, they sat on the edge of the fountain.

"This is quite beautiful," Callie said.

"The fountain was built as a tribute to the aqueducts that supplied water to ancient Rome," Jammer replied.

"I'm sure it was an engineering marvel."

Jammer laughed and Callie loved the deep, carefree sound of it. She smiled. "What's so funny?"

"It's funny because supposedly a virgin led Roman engineers to the source of the pure water."

"Once again, it takes a woman to show men where they need to go."

"You've never had any problem with telling me where

to go," he said softly. His voice was barely audible above the rushing water. She had to lean against him, making the moment intimate and romantic. "That's true," she said, rubbing her cheek against his.

Jammer slipped his arm around her, drawing her closer. Callie snaked her arm around his waist. Snuggling into the crook of his neck, she relaxed against his wide, hard chest.

"Kidding aside, this is more than a mere sculpture," Jammer said. "It's a wonderful example of Baroque art with its soft, natural lines and fantasy creatures that embody movement as the soul of the world."

Callie was stunned. Simply stunned. Jammer, who looked like he belonged in some smoky bar as a bouncer, was talking about Baroque art in such a way that it made her raise her head and study him. His eyes were a different shade of gray, like a calm, early-morning sky, content in the beginning of the day and warming from the rising of the sun.

A morning breeze ruffled his short hair, which appeared blue-black in the shortening shadows as dawn broke on the horizon. It was one of those true, genuine moments that she would always remember, like the one when he had talked about his father. A window into the real person Jammer was. The identity of the man she wanted to get to know more deeply than she would have time for.

Unexpectedly, tears pricked her eyes, and she blinked rapidly to clear them. There was no crying in black ops.

He shifted their bodies so that she was sitting between

his legs. They watched as the sun melted the gold, seeming to wash down the statues and disappear into the water until it, too, changed to aquamarine.

"It's the light and shade effects of the marble that make it seem like the clothes and hair of the statues are moving—Neptune is the one standing in the chariot being pulled by two seahorses. To the side stand Abundance and Salubrity, and around the borders of the pool are stone and carved vegetation representing the sea."

Callie got a very unique view of a piece of art from a man from whom she had expected only violence and greed. This side of him shook her foundations and crumbled her defenses all the more, until she was scrambling to find a foothold to hang on to her objectivity.

The struggle to deny her own feelings caused a pressure in her chest that grew and grew, like an inflating balloon. It crowded against her lungs, squeezed her heart, closed off her throat, pushed hard on the backs of her eyes. She had crushed it out before, time and again.

This was the paradox of being undercover. You had to *become* the person you needed to be—not role-play, not act, not pretend. She had to guard who she was from Jammer to protect her cover. It seemed ironic to try to hide anything from a man with whom she had shared the most private parts of her body, who had taken her to dizzying heights of pleasure and held her safe in his arms. She had opened her body to him, but she couldn't ever open her heart and truly share with him everything she was. Gina Callahan could do that, but Callie Carpenter couldn't.

For the first time in this crazy relationship that hurt.

"Who are you?" she asked softly, not sure if he could hear her above the rushing water that cooled her face, not sure if the moisture was tears she wouldn't acknowledge or random droplets from the fountain.

He didn't speak, but she could feel his alertness behind her, as if he wanted to tell her. Wanted to give her that insight into his character that she craved.

Finally, he said, "I'm just a cog, Gina. Just a cog."

He was wrong. He wasn't a cog, he was a linchpin, and when it was pulled, everything would come crashing down. He was her conduit to the Ghost. Her mission.

Who would have thought she would have needed that reminder? Not her. Her relationship with Jammer had been intense from the start. Those three days in Paris, as they had slaked a need for each other that became as addictive as a drug, were ones she would never forget. But she'd set up the deal with the intention of trapping the Ghost, and she had been resolved to follow through. All she could hope for in that situation would be that Jammer would get jail time, but not as much as his boss.

But then Miyagi's henchman had run her down, giving her a concussion, and she'd been out of it enough that her twin sister, Allie, had had to fill in. But Allie and Drew had failed to capture the Ghost, had lost the weapons and the money to Jammer. He had orchestrated the death of Miyagi, effectively saving her sister's life, for which Callie would always be grateful.

How to mesh this man with his international reputation for being the Ghost's muscle? It was interesting how he was always where the Ghost was supposed to be. Always the face of the organization. It made her wonder and speculate.

Jammer was much more than the Ghost's muscle. She found this intriguing, and grudgingly had to admire Jammer's intelligence.

"We'd better get going," he said as he let her go. She slid off the fountain and for an instant, in front of one of the most famous monuments in the world, she wrapped her arms around him and held him, just held on to him, breathing in his scent and enjoying the sheer physical contact.

That was the other negative side effect of being undercover—the loneliness of never really letting herself get too close.

And in her heart, she knew that even after she'd completed her mission she would always feel that loneliness, because after her mission was complete, Jammer would never hold her like this again.

7

THE ITALIAN MET THEM in a small conference room provided by the hotel. It was a quick transaction and took all of thirty minutes to complete.

As they were wrapping up, Jammer asked, "Alberto, do you have any ideas where would I get my hands on seven or eight hundred surface-to-air missiles and two planes?"

Callie closed her eyes and swore softly when Alberto regarded her quizzically.

"This information I have already given to the fair Gina. *È questo non è così?*"

Jammer looked at her as she smiled and nodded at the Italian. "Yes, you have, but I haven't had a chance to discuss it with Jammer."

"Ah, well, I must depart. Your shipment will go out this afternoon to the place you have specified." He kissed Gina's hand and exited the room with his two bodyguards.

As the door closed, Jammer turned to her. "You know

where to get the rest of the weapons? Why didn't you tell me?"

"I was checking all my contacts."

"Why do that when we have a solid lead on those weapons? It's all I need to complete the shipment."

Just then Jammer's cell rang. He answered curtly. *"Fuentes,"* he mouthed to Callie. He listened to the voice on the other end and rubbed at his temple as Fuentes's yelling rose another octave. Switching to Spanish, he said, "I am meeting my obligation and I will have everything you requested within the allotted time, which I have to point out isn't up yet." Jammer was silent again. "I don't care what rumors you've heard. I fulfill my promises and expect that everything will be to your specifications."

Fuentes's voice dropped, and Jammer ended the call shortly afterward.

"Now, who is this contact?"

"Joost Roorback," Callie said. She wasn't disappointed in Jammer's reaction.

"Son of a bitch! Three years I've been doing this and not one problem. Not one." He sat down heavily in one of the conference room chairs. "Joost fucking Roorback hates me, and the Ghost in particular. He feels that he's being dissed every time I make a buy in the Ghost's name. He's a loose cannon and a murdering, sadistic bastard. I don't want you anywhere near him."

"He doesn't hate me, Jammer. Maybe I can work with him."

"No! Out of the question. We'll find another way."

She came around the conference room table to where

Jammer was sitting. He'd worn a gorgeous gray Armani silk wool suit that darkened the shade of his eyes and easily cost ten thou if she was any judge. The silver-gray, unembellished tie made him look sleek and sophisticated. She settled her hands on his shoulders and kneaded the knotted muscles through the jacket and white silk shirt. "Okay, okay, I'm on your side. I'll keep checking with everyone I know. Jeez, don't shoot the messenger."

Jammer nodded, his features tight. "Sorry, but that man is bad, bad news."

"I've only heard rumors. I haven't had much of an opportunity to deal with him."

"Good. Steer clear. That guy's going to come to a violent end, Gina. Mark my words."

"So, I guess our trip to Italy is over. I didn't even get a chance to go to Tuscany."

Jammer swiveled the chair, cutting her legs out from under her so that she landed in his lap with an "oomph" and a giggle.

"Well, why not? When do we meet lover boy?"

Callie straightened his tie and smiled wryly, "Jammer, he's not my lover boy, and we're not supposed to see him until Friday."

"That leaves us two days. Plenty of time."

"You're serious? You want to frolic around in Florence for two days?"

"Why not? It doesn't make sense to head back to the U.S. when we'd just have to turn around and go to London. Might as well take advantage of the time we have together."

True to his word, they flew into Florence. It wasn't until they landed and got to the hotel that he told her he'd booked a bike tour around the city. Callie loved the idea.

They spent their first day doing that, then it was off to San Gimignano to a farmhouse for the night, to experience the Tuscany region and the vineyards of the area. The day was filled with nothing but wine sipping and pool lounging, until Callie felt so relaxed and refreshed she never wanted to leave.

Jammer bought a bottle of wine and a meal from the generous owners and they took it out to the terrace.

She was tipsy from the wine and warmed by the sun when she sat down to the simple but delicious fare the couple had prepared.

Jammer filled her glass and said, "This variety of wine dates back hundreds of years to Greek sailors."

"I feel as drunk as a sailor," she said softly, and they both thought that was completely hilarious.

"You know the last time I had wine with you, mister, I ended up very wet and very satisfied."

Jammer's eyes glowed, and an infectious grin split his lips. "As I recall, you didn't protest too vigorously."

"As *I* recall, I was shackled and a victim to your debauchery."

"Debauchery?"

They broke into gales of laughter over that, too.

After dinner, Callie stepped up to the railing of the terrace and appreciated the view. The panorama of the Tuscan countryside spread out before them—undulating hills topped with little terra-cotta-roofed farmhouses.

"Let's go for a walk," Jammer suggested as they left the terrace. It was getting dark, but there was a full moon and plenty of light to see where they were walking.

They soon came to a field full of red poppies gently blowing in the breeze, which carried the smell of earth and grass. Callie leaned her forearms on a fence and took in the countryside.

Jammer came up behind her, his hands encircling her waist. He kissed the back of her neck, sending spikes of pleasure down her spine. Her head reeling from the wine, she relaxed into him, breathing in his clean, sharp male scent and sighing.

"What a beautiful night and a beautiful place."

"You're beautiful, Gina. So damned beautiful."

"Is that the wine talking?" She giggled.

He chuckled and said, "No, you crazy woman, it's not. You're beautiful from the top of your silky cap of hair down to your breasts, to your long, killer legs."

"I can kill a man with my legs, you know."

He laughed softly into her neck. "I can attest to that fact."

She laughed with him, and said, "I can."

"Yeah, you're lethal, I have no doubt."

"I know moves that would shock and awe you, Jammer."

"I've already been shocked and awed by many of your moves." He kissed her ear, the laughter thick in his voice.

"Oh, you're not being serious," she said, but couldn't keep a straight face.

"As serious as I can be with a beautiful woman in

my arms and several glasses of very good wine in my system."

"Well, if we're talking about moves, Jammer, you've got some amazing ones of your own."

"Do I? Elaborate."

"Well, your mouth should be registered as a lethal weapon. It can make a woman so weak she simply can't fight back."

"What else?"

"Oh, your hands definitely need to be considered armed and dangerous, because you certainly know how to use them on defenseless victims."

"Do you mean, like this?" He cupped her breasts, gently catching her nipples between his fingers as he squeezed. A moan slipped out as she arched into his hands.

Very gently, he pushed her forward until her hands were on the fence. Huskily, he said, "Spread your legs."

Callie obeyed as he skimmed his hand from her calf up to her thigh and then under the short sundress she wore. The contact made her shudder. He planted open-mouthed kisses on her nape as his hand slid down between her legs and he curled his fingers into the sheer, lacy material of her panties. He tugged hard, ripping the insubstantial scrap of material right off her.

She gasped in shock when his seeking hand returned to her skin and the other cupped her breast. He groaned when he discovered her braless. He stroked between her legs as he continued to pull and rub her nipple.

With a low growl, Jammer thrust two fingers into her

slick core and kept on going until they were filling her up as his thumb strummed across her pulsing clit.

He pinched her nipple with just enough pressure to create a tugging, rippling sensation that spiraled down to where his other fingers were at play within her. His thumb increased its pressure, so knowing and skillful, and so intent on pushing her to dizzying heights of pleasure.

Needing an anchor from the storm about to break, she grasped the rough, slender slats of the fence. Callie threw her head back and cried out as her orgasm crested and a blissful warmth shimmied through her in waves.

Her legs turned to jelly, and just when she was certain she was going to collapse to the ground, Jammer slid inside her to the hilt, stealing her breath at the same time.

She shuddered at the feeling of being so completely filled by him, groaned as he forced his way deeper. She closed her eyes, her spine bowing as he began to move in earnest, faster, harder, stronger.

She gloried in the long groan of satisfaction she wrenched from him as she clenched her muscles tightly around him and pushed back with every last spark of need she possessed.

His hands went to her hips as he pumped into her. Her moan as her own climax built again made him growl and buck, and she cried out as he reached a place even farther inside her.

Unexpectedly, he withdrew, then flipped her around and pushed her up against the fence, catching her under the knee and lifting her leg until he could slip back inside her.

His mouth came down on hers, his tongue plunging deep and the thrust of his hips now agonizingly slow. He reached around and cradled the small of her back, grinding into her and making her throw her head from side to side as he touched some spot that sent sparks shooting all over again, and she arched, trying to keep him right there, on that spot.

"Oh, damn," she rasped, her voice soaked in pleasure. Dazed, she opened her eyes. His face was inches away from hers as he continued to thrust into her, his gray eyes so intense they burned straight to her soul, and she knew in that moment that she'd never be the same again.

He reached up and tangled his fingers in her hair, tugging her scalp back so her throat was exposed. He raked his teeth down it, the silk of his hair brushing the underside of her jaw.

Her orgasm slammed into her with the exact force of Jammer's body. She cried out his name as she convulsed around him. She arched, strung tight on the shattering pleasure, and took him over the edge with his own shout as he pistoned inside her while coming in a shuddering fury.

She held fast to him when it was over, and he held just as solidly to her, clasping her to him, even as she worked to keep her legs under her, her fingers in his hair, her face nestled in the crook of his neck.

She prayed for something that would break up

thick feeling that seemed centered in the middle of her chest.

He was still clutching her, his face buried in her hair, as if he couldn't, wouldn't ever let her go.

A huge wave of emotion blindsided her and she brought her hand up and smoothed it over his face, down the back of his shirt and over his solid, bunched shoulder muscles.

She rubbed her face against his hair and when he raised his head, she captured his mouth, his full lips warm and moist and firm against hers.

She moved her mouth over the hard edge of his jaw, peppering his face with kisses until he grasped her chin and fastened his mouth over hers again.

They kissed slowly, savoring each other. Every moment of which quenched her thirst for him in a way the most savage, intense orgasms could never do.

It started to rain lightly and they ran for the cover of the farmhouse.

WITH THEIR GLORIOUS TRIP to Tuscany behind them, Callie found their arrival in London jarring. All the people and activity hurt her eyes. Luckily, it was a quick cab ride from the airport to the Bank of London to pick up the payment.

Callie directed the cab driver to the Crowne Plaza Hotel, where they made their way directly to room 705. They knocked, and when their query was answered, they opened the door to greet Reggie.

He lounged in a chair near the window, one black-her-clad leg thrown over the side. He was a dead ringer for Billy Idol. From the blond spiked hair to his compact, muscular body to the tats, he was quite gorgeous. He even had that sneer of his full lips down to a T.

He was also one of Interpol's most competent agents. Even Callie wasn't sure how many languages he could speak. They called him "the chameleon" because he could change his character to fit into any situation. Callie had to admit that she'd come close to sleeping with him a couple of times, but had thought better of it. Too bad she hadn't been able to resist Jammer that way.

Reggie rose to his six-two height as they entered. She could feel Jammer at her back and knew that he was already on edge. That in Callie's book was dangerous. Throw in the fact that Jammer was now armed and it was even more imperative to do this deal and get out.

"Ah, Gina, my love. Is this big man your bodyguard?"

Callie rolled her eyes at him. "Cut it out, Reggie. You don't want to yank on Jammer's chain. He can so easily break it."

Reggie smiled his full dazzling grin and stopped close to her. Too close. Very gently, he ran his hand up her arm.

"Ah ducks, you know I love the adrenaline rush. So don't tease me."

She tried not to laugh as she stepped away from his touch, but she couldn't help it. Reggie was infectious. "Listen. We've got the payment, and transportation is set. So let's get on with it."

"On a tight schedule, are we?"

"Reggie, stop fooling around. This isn't a Bond flick."

"I'm so misunderstood," he said. "I think of myself as more of a canny entrepreneur than a Bond villain."

"Reggie," Callie said, more firmly.

"Well, love, I'd be the last man to disappoint you." His tone, full of sexual innuendo, only made Jammer tense more behind her. She leaned into him to show him that Reggie had no power over her.

"Then don't," she said.

"I've hit a bit of a snag. One of the ships carrying your weapons got delayed. Circumstances beyond my control."

Jammer swore under his breath, and Reggie's attention went to him. "You have something to say, wanker?"

Before Callie could even breathe, Jammer had his semiautomatic handgun out of his shoulder holster and pointed directly in Reggie's face. "Don't jerk us around, *Reggie*," he said, in that tone that sent shivers down Callie's spine.

Very gently, she put her hand on his wrist. His eyes were focused on Reggie with murderous intent. She curled her fingers around him and said softly, "We both know what this is about, and it doesn't have anything to do with delayed weapons. Maybe you should wait downstairs."

Reggie never batted an eyelash; in fact he looked bored. "Yeah, run along, bodyguard. I can take care of Gina's body for you."

"Reggie, you're not helping here," Callie said between clenched teeth.

"Ah, love, where is your sense of adventure?"

"I lost it when Jammer got peeved, and Jammer is who I care about. Get me, Reggie?"

"Yeah, I get you."

"So can we stop this pissing contest and move along?"

She waited a few tense moments. Jammer dropped his arm and stepped back. "Get on with it, Gina."

She released a sigh of relief, but Reggie just gave her a quick grin. "Tell me where you want the weapons transported and I'll do it for no extra charge."

"Deal." She passed over the payment and smiled at him. "Keep out of trouble."

He winked at her. "Can't promise that, love. Where would the fun be in that?"

Yup, a few sessions of hot sex with Reggie and she would have been on her way, with no strings attached. But it was Jammer she'd gotten entangled with, and there wasn't going to be anything easy about that.

Back in the cab and on the way to the Dorchester, where they were staying for a night, Callie turned to Jammer. "Are we going to have to talk about what just happened up there?"

He didn't look at her. "Probably," he said as the cab pulled up to the front of the hotel. Callie's phone rang—one of her contacts telling her he couldn't provide the surface-to-air-missiles or the planes Jammer needed. He'd been her last hope; they would have to deal with Joost.

By the time Callie hung up they were at the registration desk, and it took only a couple of minutes for them to check in and get into their suite.

Once inside, Callie settled herself on one of the plush sofas. Jammer stood by the window and looked out at the busy London traffic below. His face was pensive. Callie didn't relish any of the coming conversation. It was imperative that he follow her lead with her contacts. His jealousy could have been disastrous for both the mission she was on and his deal with Fuentes.

She was greedy. She wanted both the Ghost and Fuentes.

She rose from the sofa and walked over to where he stood. Still he didn't turn toward her. Was he chastising himself? Was he wishing he had taken Reggie out? Her emotions tumbled around inside her. She had known this mission would be hard. But now, standing here beside Jammer after being intimate with him on almost every level, it had gotten so damn complicated.

But her anger was mostly at herself for the position she'd put herself in. She should have told Gillian that she was compromised. That she couldn't separate herself from her emotions and stay focused on what she had to do. Now it was too late; Callie was in too deep.

"What you did was just plain stupid." She watched him carefully for his reaction. "And, Jammer, I know for a fact you're not stupid."

He looked at her, expressionless. "I'm not going to apologize for how I feel, Gina."

"Not apologize…are you crazy? I don't want your apology. I want you to make better choices. Reggie is an integral part of my business. I can't afford to alienate any of my contacts."

Jammer didn't respond right away, but went back to gazing out the window.

"Maybe you think I'm small potatoes compared to your boss, the Ghost," she told him. "Maybe it doesn't matter to you, but it matters to me."

He spun to face her, his expression still unreadable. He was so good at that, but she could recognize when his emotions were seething below the surface—Jammer became calm, much too calm. "It matters to me. Anything that concerns you matters to me. That's the fucking problem."

"Oh, great. Now I'm the problem. I'm not the one who shoved a gun in Reggie's face!"

He exploded away from the window and came up to her, his eyes blazing. "Yes, Gina. You are the problem. When we were separated, I couldn't stop thinking about you. Even now that we're together I know that as soon as this deal is done, we have to part. It messes me up. All right! Is that fine by you if I care? This situation is unbearable. If only I could let you go…"

She wanted to step back—so wanted to have the strength to step back and tell him she didn't care, that this was nothing but good sex and business. But she couldn't get the words past her lips.

"I shouldn't have shoved the gun in his face," he continued. "The way he looked at you…just pissed me off. It was irrational. Okay, is that what you wanted to hear?"

"He's a pain in the ass, Jammer. But what you showed

me up there in that hotel room was that you didn't trust me. That pisses *me* off. I've given you no reason to believe that I couldn't be trusted."

"No, you haven't," he said sincerely.

But it didn't assuage her anger. "Do you trust me?"

"It's not that. I said it was irrational. I'm not proud of it, but I've got to tell you that I would rather have taken that guy apart with my hands instead of using something as impersonal as a handgun."

"What am I supposed to do with that, Jammer? It's certainly not a way I can close this deal. We can either move forward with my contacts—and do it my way—or dissolve this right now and go our separate ways. Your choice."

She held her breath as he stood there. Without warning, he grabbed her upper arms and dragged her to him. "I want to. Part of me wants to. Then I can stop this madness. I can just get done what I need to get done. But a stronger part of me can't be without you."

Her heart twisted at his words and at the anguish in his voice. How deep did his feelings for her run? The agent in her rejoiced that he was so fully under her spell, but the woman in her melted. She totally understood words like *madness* and *irrational,* and what he'd meant about this being unbearable.

She also understood the word *hopeless.*

8

JAMMER STOOD WITH GINA'S soft flesh in his hands and cursed his inability to let this woman go. The promise of her was enough to make him want to just disappear. Just merge into the world's mass of human population and live the rest of their lives in peace.

But he couldn't. The dead souls that he had on his conscience wouldn't ever let him rest until he avenged those deaths, until Fuentes was brought to justice and the world made just a bit safer.

"I need you, Gina."

"For my contacts?"

"No," he said huskily.

He took her mouth. Right then. No preamble, no slow lowering of his lips to hers, no choice given. Just a choice made.

The surprise of it kept her motionless, but only for a second. He mentally braced himself for her to shove at him. He'd have expected that. He would have backed away, though it would have cost him. He knew then how well and truly entangled he'd become.

It had never been like this for him. He relied on instinct, on rational thought. Not on emotion and his hard-on. Or his heart. Life wasn't set up to be fair about those things, and he'd had enough of the unfair part of life.

Then she moaned, just a little guttural sound in the back of her throat. And her hands came up to fist in his hair as she pulled his mouth down even harder on hers. And returned his kiss with every ounce of intensity she had in her.

He realized there was no protecting himself from this. Or from her. And right now, he didn't want there to be.

But the cold hard facts hadn't changed. Soon Gina would be only an intense, pleasure-soaked memory.

One he would spend the rest of his days reliving.

She felt too right against him. So Jammer focused on the task at hand and ended the kiss. "Did you have any luck with your other associates? I need to wrap up this shipment."

Her silence didn't bode well. Fear and anger rolled through him again. He held her a bit tighter, then let her go.

"Oooh, given your expression and the set of your mouth, we're going to have another argument."

"Gina, this isn't a game. You play it like it is, but it isn't. Joost is not an option."

"Then there is no option. You'll have to call Fuentes and tell him you've failed to deliver on your promise."

Jammer growled in frustration. He was well aware of Gina's competency and what she was capable of. In fact, she'd be shocked and dismayed by how much he actually knew, thanks to the information he was fed about all the people he came into contact with. It made being the Ghost that much easier and so very, very successful.

But he couldn't risk his deal with Fuentes. He'd given up too much and worked too hard to get the man on the ropes. He intended to take him down. Once again he debated just severing ties with her, but he had said she could be part of the exchange. Besides, she might be able to soften up Joost and distract him from his animosity toward the Ghost.

"Jammer, I can take care of myself. It's not like I'm a noob. I've put together deals...."

"Gina, it's not about you. It's my irrationality again. Set it up and make sure that Joost understands that the Ghost will not be there. I don't want to deal with the man's bruised ego during the buy, or his refusal to sell to us."

"Jeez, I can't wait to meet this guy. He sounds like the equivalent of the soup Nazi."

Startled by this non sequitur, Jammer looked at her quizzically.

She grinned. "If we don't order just right, it'll be, 'No guns for you.'"

Jammer laughed. He gazed at her standing there, so confident and in control. Dressed in her outrageous clothes, which always seemed to work no matter what she put together. Hell, Gina could be completely naked, and somehow she'd still manage to appear as unruffled and powerful as if she was the one in charge.

He should know.

It was one of the many complexities about her that

he used as his excuse for acting so completely out of character whenever he got within five feet of her.

"You can make jokes…"

"Good ones," she said.

"Even good ones, but you know how high the stakes are. And the playing field is full of danger. All the time. Joost is a predator and very skilled at being one."

"I'd say you're better at it, Jammer, if I'm any judge of character."

"I'm a master, Gina. I've never gone head-to-head with Joost, but he doesn't scare me. But be prepared for him. He doesn't do anything conventionally. That includes the way he handles gun buys and the people involved in them."

Jammer had worked too hard to let Joost Roorback mess things up now. One way or another he would have those missiles and planes. He would prefer that Gina not be involved, but it was too late now. He was committed. He'd have to deal with her, Joost and whatever else popped up, and make sure the job got done—with him walking away the victor.

"Sometimes," Gina said, smiling like a cat ready to pounce on an unsuspecting mouse, "you have to improvise."

"I'm sure you're good at improvising. I, on the other hand, prefer to have a plan A and a plan B."

"I didn't say I didn't have any plans, just that I'm flexible enough to improvise."

"You're flexible…in many ways, but let's not put it to the test, shall we? Let's just get in, get the missiles and both go home in one piece."

"I'm all for staying in one piece, Jammer, but what happens if things don't go exactly according to plan A or plan B?"

"Then it's simple. I get mean."

"From what I've heard about Joost, that might be the only way we come out with what we want."

"We'll get what we want. I guarantee that."

With that said, he pulled her close. "I wouldn't risk you for anything, Gina. You know that, right?"

"Yes," she responded, wrapping her arms around his neck and doing his favorite thing. She settled her head on his shoulder and did this little twisting, burrowing motion that made his heart tighten.

It would have been so easy if he hadn't met her. His purpose had always been mapped out, and he'd endured three years of isolation and loneliness to accomplish it. He'd lost all that he was and had become a different person the day Fuentes had sent his goons to eliminate him and his team.

They had left him for dead, bleeding, in agony, lying among the bodies of his teammates. After the executioners were gone, he'd pulled himself to safety, but to this day, the blood of those three men and two women would remain with him until he set everything right by making their killer pay for what he'd done.

But he *had* met Gina, and he had to deal with the fact that she had come to mean more to him than any of it. If not for his guilt and his vow, he would chuck it all.

"Make the call, Gina. Let's play Joost's game our way. By our rules."

"Right, but he just won't know it."

He went back to the window as Gina contacted Joost. If Jammer had his way, Joost's right-hand guy, Dieter Fromme, would be the person he'd deal with. Dieter was easygoing and more than made up for Joost's eccentricities.

It wasn't long before Gina told him that the deal was set. They were to fly to Amsterdam tomorrow and check into the Hotel Sofitel. Someone would be in touch with them then.

"He's already started his game."

"I know. But I didn't talk to Joost. I talked to Dieter. He's the one who gave me the directions."

"Dieter is easier to deal with, but make no mistake, he protects Joost and would cut your heart out in a second if he thought you were a threat."

"Who? Little ole me?" she said, batting her eyelashes. Then her face got serious. "He wouldn't see what hit him."

Jammer could attest to that. Ever since he'd met Gina he'd been looking for the bus that had hit him.

"That means we have some time here in London. What do you want to do?" he asked.

"I say we order room service and have our own private little party."

"You don't want to see some of the sights of London?"

She grinned. "Like what?"

"Big Ben?"

She grinned that wicked grin again, and Jammer's heart started racing.

"I have my own Big Ben right here," she said, cupping

him through his trousers. "And it looks…feels like he's about to strike twelve o'clock."

"Where you're concerned, it's always twelve o'clock."

"Oh, no, that means you must be in need of repair, because clocks always have to keep the right time."

"I know how to keep the right time," he said, his voice rough now with need, and with anticipation.

"And make time, if I'm not mistaken."

Jammer chuckled as he allowed her to drag him toward the large bed in the suite. This woman had him by more than just the balls.

Something he didn't want to think about right now. He should be focusing on the buy in Amsterdam. His gut told him that they were in for trouble there, but Gina's soft hands and delectable body had other ideas.

And he was going to let her indulge every one of those ideas—hopefully for the rest of the day and into the night. Well, maybe with a break for food and hydration.

He wasn't a robot. And it was evidently clear that he was a flesh-and-blood male, because he felt completely and utterly alive with her.

A very unexpected and devastating sensation for a Ghost.

JAMMER BIT INTO THE croissant and took a sip of the delicious coffee room service had just brought him. The server didn't question him when he asked him to put the cart on the balcony, nor did he say anything when he tipped the kid a hundred bucks.

In his very proper British accent, he asked, "Will there be anything else, sir?"

Jammer shook his head and the kid left. After going a few rounds with Gina, he would have thought that sleep would have come very easily, but he hadn't been able to settle, even with her warm and sated body next to him. Maybe it was because he didn't want to get used to having her curl up next to him at night. When she was gone, he would miss that too much. Better to not indulge in that luxury so often.

He settled into a large chaise longue beneath the full moon and let the taste of the food distract his thoughts. September in London was decidedly cool and the nights even more so. He'd donned sweats and was quite comfortable with the hot coffee warming his stomach.

He was also concerned about the upcoming Amsterdam buy. He needed those surface-to-air-missiles more than he'd ever needed anything for a deal, but with Joost's unpredictable behavior, it was imperative that Jammer be able to focus on the task at hand. If he was worrying about Gina, then he wouldn't be one hundred percent effective.

Sitting there, he came to the conclusion that now that she'd set up this buy, he really didn't need her. He could pay her and she could leave.

He closed his eyes as a cloud covered the moon, his heart rolling over in his chest. It would be best to sever their ties now, though everything inside him rebelled against it.

He heard the sound of the sliding glass door and turned to find a sleep-mussed Gina blinking at him with heavy eyes. She'd donned a pair of black leggings, over which she wore a butter-yellow Henley T. Accustomed to seeing her in tulle and lace and black leather, he found the outfit made her look sweet and much too normal. Too normal for a man with so much baggage.

"What are you— Food!" She sighed as she made a beeline for the croissants. "Pour me a cup, will you?"

He smiled at her breathtaking beauty—the way her black hair shimmered, her eyes big, blue and luminous, her skin glowing in the light from the moon.

She leaned across his body, snatching at a croissant. Settling sideways on the second chaise on the balcony, she pointed at the coffee and raised her brows. He chuckled.

Instead of biting into it, she pulled off a chunk of the flaky dough and popped it in her mouth.

"Mmm, these are good."

He poured her a cup of coffee and handed it to her. Then said, "We need to talk."

The cup stopped halfway to her lips. He felt her tense beside him, and it tugged at his heart. She did that a lot, that heart-tugging thing, mostly without even trying. He didn't want that reaction from her. He wanted her to agree and just make it easier for him. Though he had to acknowledge that nothing involving Gina was either easy or simple.

Now the moment had arrived when he had to tell her to leave, and for some unexplained reason, he wasn't sure he could bear it.

He set down his cup and turned sideways, too. He took her hand, and her fingers automatically entwined with his. That small gesture sent painful yearnings through him like an electronic shock. His throat thickened.

She wasn't smiling or frowning. She looked contemplative. Normally such a look would make him want to arm himself.

"Come here," he murmured. Tugging her hand, he pulled her down next to him on the chaise. He didn't let her hand go, but absently rubbed his thumb along the side of her wrist.

"What now?" she asked, allowing him to position her against him. He loved how easily they did that—framed each other. So effortless, so damn good. "What's going on in that brain of yours?" She pressed her forehead to his.

"Too much," he said softly. "All of it bad."

"Mmm." She kissed his chin, then rubbed her cheek on his stubble. "Well, stop it." She sighed a little, and the smile that had begun to curve his lips tripped up some. "I just want to feel," she said. "Touch, taste, sound, smell…" She tipped her head back and looked between the trees out in front of the hotel. But the moon had been swallowed by clouds again, leaving her upturned face in deep shadow. "But I guess I'm not going to get to do that, am I?" She sighed and returned her eyes to him. "So, let's have it."

"I'd rather talk about the touching and tasting part."

She smiled slightly. "Me, too. But the stubborn realist in me apparently won't let go. So spill. What do you have to say to me?"

He held her gaze for a long minute, then sighed

himself. She was right, no matter how badly either of them would like to think otherwise. "In the morning, you should book yourself a flight back to the States, to your destination of choice. I'll go on to Amsterdam and complete the deal. It's really over, Gina. We both know that we can't stay together. It was never your intent, that's for sure. You said as much in Napa. So let's not prolong it. I can have your cut wired to your bank. I just need—"

Gina raised her palm. "That's it? Our business is done because you say it is?"

"Yes."

"This isn't about the deal."

"You fulfilled your end of the bargain. You got me the contacts."

"That's right, I did. I also don't quit in the middle. I'm following through on this one. This is a rehash of the argument we had before. You're trying an end run around me. I don't like it." She looked past his shoulder to the street below as a black taxi drove by, shattering the sudden silence.

"I don't want you in the way."

"Oh, really?"

He swore under his breath, hearing how the words sounded. "That's not what I meant. You know me and you know I only meant that you distract me too much."

She didn't pursue that line of thought, but he could tell from her contemplative expression that it was only going to be a matter of time. She'd already delved a little into his life. He liked that she was curious about him, that she'd want to know more. But he was unable to give her the real details—all of them, anyway.

But for a split second he wanted to. He wanted to unburden himself—his motives, his overall plan. But there was just too much at stake, too much danger involved with revealing who he really was, what he was really doing.

He wanted to grab her shoulders and shake her, make her understand that they weren't actually a team here. He cringed at that word. Never had he intended to team with anyone again. His reactions, his very motivation was to shun involving another person in this terrible and dangerous game he was playing.

Yet in his heart, that's what it was. They *were* a team. But his head knew they were something totally different. Something he couldn't define or categorize.

Her defiant pose lasted another moment, then her shoulders dipped slightly as she pulled away from him and stood up. "Okay, Jammer. Have it your way. I'm not going to wait until the morning, if you don't mind. I'm leaving now." Her tone was still defensive, even if her posture said otherwise.

It was as if the light went out of his life—just died, and he felt that big chasm open up inside him. The one that Gina filled to the brim. His throat closed and he forced himself to turn away from her. He wanted to shout his pain to the full moon, but kept his mouth closed. He'd kept his mouth closed, his identity hidden, for three long years, all for one goal. He couldn't fail to achieve that goal or he would surely become the Ghost he pretended to be, consumed from the inside out by his guilt and his desire for vengeance.

He couldn't rest until Fuentes had paid, one way or the other. He wouldn't be a good companion or anything else for Gina.

"Thank you for all your help."

"Jammer, go to hell," she said, softly but firmly.

The door closed with a snap and he picked up his cup, only to find that his coffee was as stone-cold as his heart.

CALLIE PACKED HER BAGS haphazardly, the Gina clothes flung inside in a fit of pique. Damn him. Why did he have to get all noble on her? He was supposed to be a fucking gunrunner, for Pete's sake. Why did he care about her? Why? It made her life twice as difficult. Her eyes filled suddenly and without warning. Her hands trembled as she turned and sat down on the edge of the bed to get herself under control. It wouldn't do to lose her cool now. She was a government agent—a Watchdog agent—and she was made of better stuff than this.

No way was she going to let this fall apart. She couldn't. Her plan just had to be altered a bit. She was going to Amsterdam whether Jammer liked it or not.

She'd just be going there separately. Once the deal was complete, she'd figure out a way to worm herself back into the final exchange. She'd have to.

She called down to the desk to have her luggage picked up, and bit her lip. Should she try one more time to repair her undercover mission, or go a different route?

She decided to let him stew. Let him miss her, because although she wouldn't acknowledge it before, Jammer had a serious jones on for her. It was something she could use to her advantage. She grabbed a cab to the airport and paid as she exited.

Distracted by the situation with Jammer, Callie noticed the dark sedan only when a man stepped out in front of her. He ordered her in heavily accented English to get inside.

She declined.

That's when three other doors opened and three other men climbed out.

Oh, crap.

She brought down the first man with a move her brother, Max, had shown her. Although the second man got a few good hits in, she took him out with a combo Drew had taught her.

But when the third pulled a gun on her, she had no choice.

"Who are you and what do you want?"

"Americans. Always kicking the butt first and asking the questions second."

Was this guy for real? Was he making a joke? If so, it was most definitely at her expense.

"Joost wants some leverage against the Ghost. You, I'm afraid, are that leverage."

"You're wrong. We're just business associates. He doesn't give a damn about me."

"That's too bad for you, then, isn't it, *mijn vriend*."

"I'm not your friend."

"That is also too bad for you."

IN THE MORNING, Jammer packed up. He was feeling the loss of Gina acutely, but he pushed it aside and boarded the plane for Amsterdam.

The flight was short, just one hour and change, but once he landed in Schiphol Airport, the passport lines were long and it took him a bit to get through.

He grabbed a cab and found himself at the Sofitel. Now it was a waiting game.

When his phone rang three hours later, Jammer answered with a clipped hello. He was at the whim of a conscienceless bastard. What had he expected? Courtesy?

"Go out to the front of the hotel. There's a car waiting for you."

Jammer immediately left the room. Once this deal was complete, he'd be going back to Napa to wrap up all the transportation and storing details, and then off to Colombia to reap the fruits of his labor.

The only piece of information he needed from Fuentes was where and when the Defensores de la Libertad would be assembled for an easy and complete takedown.

It was fitting. An ambush for the ambusher.

At the street, Jammer looked for the car. He saw a black Mercedes parked at the curb, and refrained from rolling his eyes; just about every bad guy in every movie that involved international espionage drove a black Mercedes.

The door opened for him. Jammer settled inside and sighed when a blindfold was placed over his eyes. It was all part of the Joost dog and pony show.

He endured the ride without comment, derisive as the ones in his head were. He wanted to get in, get the goods, close the deal and move on.

Just like he'd moved on with Gina?

In the dark behind this blindfold wasn't where he wanted to be. It gave him much too much time to think about Gina, the warmth of her skin, her witty and often amusing comebacks, her out-there personality and her wicked grin.

Finally the car came to a halt. He began to remove the blindfold, but was stopped.

"Not yet."

He allowed one of the errand boys to steer him toward his meeting place with Joost.

When his blindfold was removed, he found himself standing outside a windmill, one that was evidently used as a sawmill. He could hear the saws going in the background and wondered briefly if Joost had made an investment in a legitimate business, just as Jammer himself had.

One of Joost's goons shoved him in the back, and they entered the main part of the mill. They passed an office without stopping, and ended up in an open area beyond it. No one but Joost was there. Jammer wondered all of a sudden where Dieter was. Dieter was never far from Joost's side.

"Jammer, *mijn vriend*."

"Joost. Are we ready to do this? As soon as we seal the deal and I take a look at the merchandise, we can both be on our merry way."

"Ah, Americans, ever the businessmen. There is never the time for preliminaries."

"Preliminaries? What do you want to do? Dine together? I'm on a tight schedule, as I'm sure Ms. Callahan told you."

"Yes, Ms. Callahan did give this information to me. She was very clear."

As soon as Gina's name was mentioned, Jammer got a tight feeling in his gut. Joost's eyes took on a knowing gleam, one that did not bode well for either Jammer or Gina.

"Often we have made deals. Is this not so?"

"We have. It's been very profitable for everyone concerned."

"*Ja.* That is true, but profits are not all that concern me. It is the constant disrespect from your employer that has caused this concern."

Jammer wanted to groan and rub his temple, but didn't. It was important to remain unaffected and in control. "Joost, the Ghost has employed me to handle these situations. It's my job—"

Looking bored, Joost raised his arm and snapped his fingers.

That's when Jammer found out exactly where Dieter was. He came out of the office, his meaty hand clamped around Gina's upper arm.

He could see that her lip was cut and she had a doozy of a black eye. He could only imagine how bad the other guys' were.

"Join us, Ms. Callahan. We were just talking about your associate's employer. Ah, but now that I see how he looks at you, I'm convinced that you are much more than his associate. *Ja.*"

"What do you want, Joost?" Jammer asked.

His smile was anything but sweet. "You will contact your boss and you will tell him that if he wants this shipment, he can close the deal himself."

Jammer looked at Gina. His soul had awakened the day she'd opened that hotel room door. She hadn't slid into his life; she'd come rushing like a storm, dragging emotions from him he'd thought were buried too deep to revive. But they were there, just beneath his skin, and there simply wasn't anything he wouldn't do for her, even break a vow.

At Jammer's inactivity, Joost snapped his fingers again, and Dieter pulled a gun from inside his leather jacket and placed it against Gina's temple.

"There's no need for threats, Joost. I don't have to call my boss."

"Why is this?"

"He's already standing right here."

"You?"

"I am the Ghost."

9

CALLIE JUST STOOD THERE, Dieter's gun still pressed against her temple.

She heard the words. Saw them come out of Jammer's mouth. But she couldn't comprehend them. They were a foreign language she had never heard before.

Jammer was the Ghost.

The man she had sworn to bring to justice was the man she'd been sleeping with all this time. But surely Jammer was only saying that because he thought Gina was in danger. It couldn't be true.

But as their eyes met across the room, she knew it. Knew he was telling the truth.

"*Ja.* This is a surprise, but it is as I suspected. Why the ruse?"

Jammer shrugged. "To stay under the radar."

"Like the Batman?"

"Yes, like Batman," he agreed.

Callie tensed, readying herself for action. She had every intention of surviving this encounter. She was going to arrest the Ghost no matter who he was. She met Jammer's eyes and no words were spoken, but it was as if they could speak to each other's souls. He was prepared to act, as well. She knew Jammer wasn't leaving here without securing those weapons. The pressure tautened as Joost studied him. Just when Callie thought everything was going to dissolve into chaos, Joost's barking laughter broke the silence.

The man threw up his hands. "Then all is forgiven. I love the Batman. Dieter, let her go."

The cold metal disappeared from her temple, but Callie couldn't move.

"Gina, come over here," Jammer said softly. "Now."

She got her feet to function and she went to him.

Then he did something that made her heart jump. He stood in front of her, effectively using his big body as a human shield. Up close, she could see how pale the skin was on the nape of his strong neck, the coiled muscles that belied how worried he was for her safety, and her emotions went wild. She was mad and touched at the same time. She just didn't know what to do with it all. Her throat got tight and that only set off her anger again. Could she really blame anyone but herself? She had told herself what she was doing wasn't exactly a good idea. Sleeping with Jammer had been an irresponsible indulgence. His charisma and her inability to control the desire she felt for him were her downfall. And here it was in living Technicolor.

This man who was coolly negotiating an arms deal was the elusive villain numerous agencies would kill to get their hands on.

She mentally slowed her breathing, realizing that she was going to hyperventilate if she didn't get control of herself.

The jumble of emotions she felt only added to a terrible confusion undercutting her confidence. Callie was furious that she hadn't seen this herself, and at the same time had a heartfelt need to wrap her arms around him and hold on until this confusion ended. But then anger burned through her. Oh no, this made everything ten times worse.

Mercifully, Jammer finished with Joost quickly. All in all, the exchange had gone a lot better than they'd anticipated.

In parting Joost said, "I commend you for your choice in a woman. It will take a strong man to handle her."

"No one handles Gina, Joost."

Even with all the tension, and the fact that she had come very close to death, Callie smiled. It wasn't long before they were in the Mercedes and at the Sofitel.

Inside, she expected Jammer to yell at her, curse her for not returning to the States as he'd asked. It would have been reasonable. It would have made sense.

So when the hotel room door closed and he leaned against it, saying nothing, she took the offensive. "This is your fault, you know. They got me at the airport. I tried to fight them off, but one of them got the drop on me. I had no choice. It seems that Joost planned this to force you to contact the Ghost."

"My guess is that your plane ticket wasn't for someplace in the U.S."

She faced him squarely, her eyes locked with his, his

handsome, impassive face giving nothing away. "No. But, again, your fault. If you hadn't cut me out of the deal halfway through, I wouldn't have been at the airport by myself. I intended to finish the negotiation and in the process make a new contact."

"Business. That's always what it is for you?"

She marched up to him and grabbed him by the lapels of his suit. She needed to do something physical or she was going to come out of her skin. The stakes had risen and the situation she found herself in had just gotten that much worse.

How was she going to reconcile her damn feelings for this man when she had to snap those handcuffs on him, face him in court? When he'd just done something so shocking, so unselfish, for her?

She represented the law. There had to be justice and accountability, but nothing was simple when emotions were involved. Why couldn't he have turned out to be an asshole instead of a man she admired? It wasn't about the danger now or the illicitness of their affair; it was about her strong attachment to him, stronger than she wanted to admit.

He was the Ghost!

"What else is there, Jammer? Or should I call you the Ghost? That was a nice tidbit of information to drop on me!"

He seized her by her shirtfront and pulled her close to his face. His eyes were hard as diamonds, his mouth full and tight. In them she saw his fear and something else she couldn't name, wouldn't name. It would have knocked her back if he didn't have such a tight grip on her shirt. "I wouldn't have had to drop it at all if you had just done what I asked. You have no idea how much this complicates my life, how much is at stake. But you were more interested in business then preserving your own life."

"Look, I can take care of myself. I would have come up with something to get myself out of that jam. But you're the one keeping secrets, it seems."

"Doesn't everyone?"

She froze inside at his look—almost as if he knew she was undercover. But that wasn't possible. If he did know, he would have taken her out of this charade from the beginning.

His mouth covered hers, hot and demanding her to respond. She couldn't help herself. The compulsion to soothe his fear and panic came from a deep well in her; until this moment she hadn't known she possessed that much emotion. The sacrifice he'd just made for her spoke volumes.

"I can't lose you. Not that way."

His words made her throat cramp, and it hit home hard that one day she was going to be without him. It almost made her want to defect to the dark side. Made her frantic to think of a way to get herself and him out of this situation. But she knew there was nothing she could do. She was ensnared in a trap of her own making.

She was much too dedicated to the vow she'd taken to serve and protect the United States, and rationally, she knew it was panic forcing her to think about treason. She would do what had to be done. No matter how much it hurt.

And it was going to hurt so bad.

"Then let's not waste the time we have."

JAMMER DIDN'T KNOW WHAT he was going to do about Gina. There was no going back to the way he'd been before he'd met her. Her words slammed into him and sent his body into lock and load. So easily.

Her hands slid around his neck. Her face was pensive, soft with desire, her eyes dark with secrets and the pain that came with them. He wished that he could take that look from her eyes, but he couldn't. He'd already crossed the line. It was going to be bad enough when he had to clean up the mess he'd made. He teetered on the edge of revealing to her who he really was, and the dangerous and clandestine game he played with a powerful and dangerous foe, but he curbed it. It would jeopardize the outcome. Gina had to stay in the dark for now. She was as safe as he could make her.

She pulled his willing mouth down to hers. He tried for tenderness, for less than what he was feeling, but it wasn't possible, not with Gina. Not with the excitement she generated with just existing.

He couldn't live without her, without this, he thought, closing his arms snugly around her, one palm molding her curves and the other slipping under her shirt. She opened his pants, boldly driving her hand inside, and a bubble settled over them, encased them in heat, her kiss setting off the wild lick of flames down his body. Gentleness vanished and they were tearing at each other, at their clothes.

He grabbed her back, his mouth trailing hotly down

her throat. He paused long enough to strip off her shirt, toss it with his before his lips closed over her nipple. He drew it into the heat of his mouth as if trying to devour her, his tongue circling and flicking.

Gina shimmered with desire and he drank it in, the scent of her, the way she tasted him as if she never would again, her lithe, sexy body flexing as his hands roamed over her roughly, almost desperately.

He pushed her jeans down; she tried kicking them off without stopping the kiss. Then in a frantic scramble they stripped, and she was back in his arms, his hand sweeping down her body and between her thighs.

"Oh, Jammer," she breathed, and with her arms around his neck, she hopped up and clamped her legs around his hips.

"What have you done to me?" she whispered, her voice carrying pain.

He worried her mouth, cradling her behind, and pulled her to him. His erection slid wetly against her center, and Jammer loved the way her breath hitched.

"The same thing you've done to me," he growled.

She nibbled his ear, his throat, and they both trembled with anticipation of him pushing inside her.

"You're not leaving my side until this is over, Gina— Oh damn, you feel good."

"Finally you see it my way," she said, her breath coming in gasps.

"Trouble is your middle name." From behind, he dipped his fingers deeper.

"I'll have it legally changed if you stay this close to me.… Oh, gosh, don't stop doing that."

"I can't," he whispered as he sank to the carpet, stroking her, and she grew more breathless, thrusting against him as she followed him to the floor.

She managed to say, "The bed...." Her hand closed over his erection, eliciting a dark, heavy groan.

"Can't stop." He pushed into her palm, his mouth rolling over the flesh he could reach.

She rose up on his thighs, guiding him, teasing him mercilessly as she rocked on his erection. Her smile was sinful, her fingers gliding over the tip of him. He couldn't wait any longer, and leaned her back onto the carpet.

He entered her and for a moment held still, her hands on his face, her gaze locked with his. Emotions swelled, tightening his chest, his heart pounding so hard he swore she could feel it. The image of Gina with a gun to her head suddenly flashed in his mind—he'd almost lost her. The terror of it made him realize his need for her went beyond this frenzied desire, beyond his mission.

"This is so good, I don't want it to end," she whispered, and arched up to shred him with a kiss.

Jammer quaked with the savageness of it, her impatience, and without will, he moved. Gina pushed back, her heat flexing around him, a tight, firm lock on more than his body. He laced his fingers with hers, as if being joined together wasn't enough. She smiled up at him as he withdrew and sank into her again. She rolled her hips in a devastating maneuver that almost made him come. When she quickened, he knew he wouldn't make it, and then it didn't matter. Her mouth was on his, her body pumping with his, and she stopped kissing him long enough to whisper, "I think you can *handle* me quite easily."

Jammer chuckled and scooped her off the floor, onto his lap. Her eyes flared at the slick, wet length of him and she rocked, using her weight to drive him to the floor. She laughed at his startled look and said, "Well, maybe not."

His response was cut off as she rode him, leaving him completely, only to shove back, her blue eyes wicked and full of her power. She knew what she was doing to him. Unhinging him. *She had him. She truly had him cold.*

Energy rocked and pulsed—around them, between them. He could almost taste it on her mouth. Jammer sat up, their motions primal and raw. She was on the brink, her body flexing around him, clawing him.

"Gina, oh, damn."

"I know."

He flipped her on her back and his hips thrust uncontrollably. The explosion ripped, pushing them across the floor. She bit her lip to keep from screaming, but Jammer swallowed her cries as her slick, wet muscles pawed him, drew him with her. Tumbling into pleasure. He watched her ride the eruption, savored the sight of pure satisfaction shimmering through her. Gina left nothing to chance, taking it all and glowing with ecstasy.

He wasn't sure how long they lay there on the floor, panting and trying to breathe around the pleasure. He looked up into her eyes, then away, afraid of what she would see there. All this time, every step, action, kiss and embrace, had led him right here. To this moment.

He closed his eyes tight and sighed heavily, thinking about what he would have to sacrifice for a low-life bastard who didn't deserve the time of day. Fuentes would get his just deserts, but Jammer still wouldn't be free of the past that haunted him.

He would have to sacrifice Gina.

He opened his eyes and she was staring up at him like a woman dazed. She lifted her hand to his mouth, touching his lips as if she could absorb him into her body.

He would have been able to endure that look, even that touch, but what undid him was the tremble in her fingers. With a soft exhalation of air, he groaned, the agony of wanting almost too much for him to bear.

He grabbed her wrist and placed several kisses against the palm of her hand. She cupped his face, running her thumb over his mouth once more, then delved into his hair and urged him down to her mouth.

Her lips trembled, too, and he kissed her softly, gently, cherishing her response.

He got off her and picked her up in his arms. She smiled at him. "My Prince Charming."

For her sake, he laughed, because that's what she wanted him to do. Walking over to the bed, he cradled her against him as he pulled the covers off and sank down with her into the softness.

Then he curled around her and held her against him because he needed to. He knew he had a phone call to make and pressing problems to deal with, but he was going to take this time.

Time that would soon grow very short.

"Where do we go from here, Jammer?" She held his gaze intently.

"Tell me something about yourself—anything."

"Why…" Her brow furrowed, as if she just couldn't figure him out. When he did reveal to her who he was, she would be surprised, but would she forgive him for keeping his identity a secret? Or would she be fuming mad?

He shrugged. "Because I want to know. I just want to know."

Her hand went to his biceps and she wound her fingers over him. A small smile curved her lips and her eyes met his. "My guilty pleasure is martial arts B movies."

"Ah, a peek into the dangerous woman's psyche. You like all that physical stuff, huh?" he asked, bumping her hip. "Is that why you're in this line of work? So you can live out your guilty pleasure?" He smoothed his hand down her back in a slow caress, enjoying the feel of her soft skin.

"I'm not sure," she said with a laugh, "but I do get to kick butt on a regular basis, which makes me happy. I just don't shout *'Hiya!'* when I do it."

He laughed and pulled her close. "Next time you kick ass, and I'm anywhere near the vicinity, you will shout *'Hiya!'*"

"Is that a requirement for staying with you until this deal is over?"

He didn't answer. He was torn—torn up inside and torn by his need to protect her. But he had to be realistic.

She sighed. "Do I have to go through how it was all your fault that I ended up compromised, or are you going to give in easily? Don't make me shout *'Hiya!'* at you."

"It would almost be worth it. The part about you being a distraction hasn't changed."

"So, worry about me while I'm right beside you. You can allay all your fears and have me, too."

"I like that course of action," he said. For a moment they lay together without speaking.

The silence was soothing, and holding her was a boon to his soul. Finally her breathing slowed and he knew she was asleep.

It was time to pay the piper.

JAMMER LEFT A SLEEPING Gina. Donning a pair of jeans and a shirt, he slipped out of the hotel room and went down to the busy, noisy lobby.

He'd screwed up royally. Completely. Now came the damage control. He dialed the number and waited until the line was picked up.

"Since you're calling me at this hour, it must be important." The voice was slurred and concerned.

Jammer didn't sugarcoat it. There was no time to break the information gently. "My identity has been breached."

Now the voice was wide-awake. Jammer heard the rustle of blankets and a light being snapped on. "That's not possible. Only you and I know that you're—"

In a voice that sounded much calmer than he felt,

Jammer said, "No, not my real identity, the Ghost identity."

"How did this happen? Who is involved?"

Jammer gave him the story, leaving nothing out. The silence on the other end of the line stretched, but Jammer was used to it. His partner needed time to think about the next move.

"All right, we'll snatch up Roorback and Fromme and put them on ice until you've finished with Fuentes. I'll set that in motion as soon as I get off this phone."

"What do we do about Gina Callahan?"

"What do we do with an undercover Watchdog agent who has the knowledge that the very man everyone is after has now just blown his cover?"

Jammer rubbed at his temple. "Yeah. I think I can persuade her to keep the information to herself. My guess is that I'm her target, but if she can bag Fuentes in the process, she'll be happy to wait just a little bit longer."

"We'll neutralize her in a different way than we planned. Leave that up to me. She is still unaware that you know she's Callie Carpenter, correct?"

"Yes, I've managed not to reveal that information. It would require explanations that I can't give her right now."

Jammer looked out at the people milling about the hotel—checking in at the front desk, going to dinner and moving in and out of the elevators. He sat down on one of the sofas in the lobby, suddenly exhausted.

"I understand why you revealed the Ghost's identity.

You had no choice. Letting a government agent die is not what we're about."

"I'm aware of that. If anything had happened to her, I would go mad and that would effectively screw up this whole thing anyway."

"You in that deep, then?"

The question was not unexpected, and it was just common sense to reveal everything. This situation couldn't get any worse. "I'm afraid so. I intend to keep her with me until this is all over, so square that up."

"I think that's the best solution at this point. At least with her by your side, you can watch her. Let me get moving on these problems. I'll call you back when they're handled. Jammer, stay focused. We're almost to ground zero."

Jammer sighed. "It doesn't change anything for us. I still can't have a relationship with anyone and you know it. We both do."

For the first time since Jammer had met the man on the other end of the line, he heard compassion in his voice. "If she's willing to go under with you...?"

"You think I would subject her to the hell that I've had to go through these last three years?" Jammer hissed. "I can't ask her to give up everything like I did. She has a family."

"You have one, too."

"It's not the same. I'd be asking her to choose between us, and that just isn't fair. I had no other choice to make. I was already dead. I made my choice based on what happened to me. It was the right thing to do. Fuentes has to be taken out of action."

"Yes, it's a tough situation you're in. I admire what

you're doing. We wouldn't have even gotten this close to realizing our plan if it wasn't for what you sacrificed. When we lost those agents… Even though we found you alive, I was incensed the mission had gone so wrong."

"I bought into it. It was my decision. Their deaths are on both of us."

"And now we have a real chance at making it right. So much is at stake—that's why it's critical to keep all this top secret. No one—I mean no one—can know."

"I've kept my part of the bargain. I agreed to the rules."

"I believe it's what's protected you all this time. Everyone—other agents, their agencies, even the president—was kept in the dark. It was our plan that the other agencies would perpetuate your cover for you. The disappearance of a few people all worked in our favor. But now those agencies are getting serious about bringing you in. So I'll have to break protocol and reveal information to the director of Watchdog that I wouldn't normally reveal."

"Do what you have to do to buy me more time. Fuentes is so close to prison orange. He has to pay, or this has all been for nothing."

"And the Watchdog agent? Would you risk it for her?"

"No. I couldn't and still be able to live with myself—or look her in the eye."

"I'll be in touch."

RUSSELL STANFORD, the director of the DEA, lay back on the pillows. He'd never had a case like this one. It was unique, and the whole burden of the plan fell on his shoulders. It had been his idea. Of course, Jammer had leaped at the chance to bring Fuentes to justice.

Even now, Russell wouldn't let himself think of what he had done to protect the whole operation. Sometimes justice required a hefty price, and someone had to pay it.

"Russell, is everything all right?" his wife asked in a sleepy voice.

"No," he replied. "I need to talk to the director of Watchdog."

"I hope you're not in the doghouse," she said with a chuckle.

That's why he loved her. She didn't mind being woken up in the middle of the night, she endured his sometimes unreasonable working hours and she was always there to support him. A true patriot's wife.

"Go to sleep, sweetie. I'll just be a minute." Russell bent over and kissed her, then turned off the light. He went into the study for privacy and so he wouldn't disturb his wife.

The first few phone calls he placed were to a couple of agents who excelled in what Russell liked to call a bag and gag. After indicating that Joost Roorback and Dieter Fromme must be kept on ice for an indefinite span of time, he then placed his next call to Gillian Santiago, director of Watchdog and the one who was going to keep Callie Carpenter on a short leash. She was a formidable woman and an excellent director. She would understand that the DEA wouldn't ask for dispensation unless it was due to dire circumstances. It looked as if he wasn't the only one who was going to lose sleep tonight.

10

"ARE YOU GOING TO wear that on the plane?" Jammer asked.

Callie went to a mirror to check out her backside, trying to see what he was talking about. "Why, do I have a rip or something?" The denim skirt she wore was short and tight, made out of spandex. The hot-pink top covered her torso, but bands of see-through material played peekaboo with her skin.

"Or something," he said, looking her up and down and shaking his head.

"What? It covers me," she said with a smirk.

His eyebrows rose. "In all the right places."

"If anything, it might get us through the customs line a little bit faster."

Callie's phone rang and she glanced at the number. Answering, she said, "Tina, you can't believe what Jammer just said about my outfit." Callie had been trying to reach her boss ever since she had woken up this morning. It was 3:00 a.m. in Washington, D.C., but Callie knew that Gillian would be anxious to hear about the information she possessed about the Ghost.

"Can you get away?" Gillian asked.

She sounded very tired, but fatigue came with the job. "I only have a moment. We're getting ready to fly back to Napa. I've been trying to get in touch with you."

"I'm sorry about that. I've been on the phone with the DEA," Gillian said.

"I have much more pressing news."

"Gina, I'll take the bags downstairs and check out. We still have enough time for you to talk to your sister," Jammer said as the bellboy rapped on the door.

She chatted about Amsterdam as the bellboy efficiently stacked their bags on the trolley. He and Jammer left the room.

"Okay, he's gone. You'll never guess who Jammer really is."

"I hate to steal your thunder, but I already know he's the Ghost."

Callie paused in pulling on a short black boot. "What? How is that possible? I just found out last night, and the only other two people in the room were Joost Roorback and Dieter Fromme."

"Yes, that is true, but the DEA director called me himself. They had an agent in the organization who overheard."

She pulled on the other boot. "Is that going to be a problem for us?"

"No, but you can't arrest him until the Fuentes deal is done. The DEA has an operation going and they don't want to jeopardize the agent they have in the field."

"So we have to back off."

"Don't worry, the DEA director promised me there would be enough of the Ghost to go around. Just don't lose him. Stick to him like a second skin."

Callie smiled at Gillian's words. Her boss had no idea how close Callie was to the Ghost.

"Oh, and, Callie, watch out. The Ghost is notorious for eliminating anyone who knows his identity. Roorback and Fromme have disappeared."

"What?" Callie sank down on the unmade bed, her heart pounding.

"Yup, off the face of the earth. It takes some doing to make people disappear without a trace. I don't want to lose one of my best agents. If it gets hot, abort and return to D.C. Let the DEA take over."

Callie stiffened. "I don't think so. I have lost this guy too many times to let someone else nab him."

Gillian chuckled at Callie's stiff tone. "I'm not going to lie and tell you this wouldn't be a feather in Watchdog's cap. But, Callie, I'm serious. Protect yourself first."

"Yes, ma'am."

"Don't get smart with me," Gillian said, and added quietly, "Be careful."

"I didn't take the job to be careful, Gillian, but I won't be reckless, either." It was way too late for that, anyway. That advice would have served her much better if she'd heeded it the first time she'd ever laid eyes on Jammer, the sinfully sexy bastard.

She exited the hotel room and met Jammer in the lobby.

"Did you have a nice chat with your sister?" Jammer asked as she came abreast of him.

"Yes, I did," Callie replied, easily letting the lie roll off her tongue. She couldn't stop thinking about Joost and Dieter. Had he killed them to keep them quiet? It was hard to reconcile this man with the reputation. There was something about him that suggested he wasn't a cold-blooded killer, but what had happened to those two thugs?

He checked the slim Rolex on his tanned wrist. "She's up at 3:00 a.m.?"

Was there suspicion in his voice? "Yes, she's a party girl. Doesn't get to bed sometimes until dawn."

Jammer nodded. With his hand settled comfortably against the middle of her back, he ushered her out of the hotel and into the waiting cab.

"So what is the next step? When do you deliver?"

"Not for a few more days. Thanks to you and Roorback, I'm ahead of schedule."

The airport was as crowded as she suspected, so it took them quite a bit of time to get through customs and security.

Three flights and seventeen and a half travel hours later they landed in San Francisco. Shortly after that, they were back at Jammer's Napa Valley winery.

Jammer dropped the luggage at the front door, then grabbed their toiletry cases and her hand. "Time to get some sleep," he said with a yawn.

"Really?" she inquired.

"Yes, sleep. We're both exhausted. I'll need to be fresh for the harvesting that's going on here. I have details to handle regarding the shipment for Fuentes and travel arrangements for our trip to Colombia." He pulled her forward.

"I'm all for some rest. I'm beat."

"Good."

As they climbed the stairs, Callie asked, "So did you have Joost and Dieter killed?" She had to ask. It had been on her mind the whole trip back to California.

Everything about him went utterly still for a split second, as if her question had literally stopped him cold. But he recovered so quickly, Callie almost convinced herself she had imagined the response. He turned to look at her. "How did you hear about that so soon?"

"It's a natural assumption. I know how you operate, Jammer. Everyone does. Those who find out the Ghost's identity quickly disappear."

"I did what was necessary to protect my alter ego. The Ghost needs to remain a secret. It's the way it works."

"Why is that?"

"For one, it keeps me out of prison. You can't arrest someone who doesn't exist. For another, it's also very difficult to find someone who doesn't exist. Jammer is a good cover. I'm just the Ghost's muscle. No one usually pays me much attention."

"I think it's a brilliant idea. Sure had me fooled." She scooted past him on the stairs, remembering where his room was.

"I can't have anyone knowing who I really am." He caught up to her and followed closely as they moved down the hall.

She turned to him, her tone serious. "Who are you?"

He yawned again and grinned at her, his smile bright in the dimness. "A tired man."

She let him duck the question, because soon enough he was going to have to reveal who he really was. When she snapped handcuffs around his wrists. Confusing and conflicting emotions twisted and writhed in her chest, the pressure building like a steam engine.

"I know who the Ghost is. What are you going to do about me?" she asked, poking him in the chest. Outside they heard thunder rumble.

They hadn't quite made it to the bedroom and Jammer hadn't had a chance to turn on a light. The only illumination came from the moon, which was quickly getting swallowed up by clouds outside the wide windows. He suddenly pushed her up against the wall.

His gaze, hot and magnetic, caught her, his dark eyes glittering. "I don't think you're going to tell anyone my secret."

Callie looked up into his face and felt her heart break. She'd already told her boss he was the Ghost. Already breached his trust. But, she rationalized, Callie wasn't Gina Callahan and she wasn't an arms dealer. She also wasn't deeply, hopelessly, in love with the Ghost. All she had to do was repeat that to herself over and over again until it sank in.

"Why wouldn't I tell anyone?"

Lightning flashed in the distance, casting his hard, handsome face in silver. "Because you're not a blabbermouth, and you will keep the secret because it's to your advantage. Now you have some leverage over me."

"Do I?"

Dropping the toiletry cases, he leaned down, meeting her at her level, his nose almost touching hers, his eyes a shocking gray as if the storm that gathered outside now raged in his eyes, and said, "You know you do, Gina." He grinned an unholy grin, his eyes shining like hard granite in the shadows. "You must know you do," he whispered, his whiskey-hoarse voice scraping her nerve endings like a rasp.

As his lips found her throat and he began to kiss her with teasing little nips, Callie closed her eyes. She wanted to savor the feel of his mouth against hers and to compose herself, because, damn the bastard, he was right.

"There's a part of you that wants to keep me safe from harm, a part that wars with self-preservation and your own goals. But it's there," he murmured, his deep voice thick with words he couldn't say.

"I thought—" She broke off at the breathless sound of her own voice, cleared her throat and tried again. "I thought we were going to bed to sleep."

He chuckled wickedly against her neck, sliding a hand up and down her upper arm, his thumb brushing seductively against the side of her breast.

"You're right. I'm getting sidetracked." His expression grew serious, intense, as he stared down at her, and a tremor went through her. This Jammer looked like a dominant male, a predator, capable of anything.

Callie shook her head, sidestepping him as he moved away from her and retrieved their toiletries from the floor. She was amazed at his ability to go from teasing to serious, then seductive, then teasing again. It was almost more unnerving than his ability to make her want him.

He lifted his hand and cupped her cheek, the fire in his eyes softening to tenderness.

She leaned into him as his arm slipped around her. Together they went into the bathroom to clean up and get ready for bed.

Was that why she wanted to save him, protect him, find some way out of this tangled, impossible mission? Because Jammer treated her with the utmost care?

They quickly undressed and crawled beneath the covers. He immediately pulled her to his side, and she moved willingly into his arms.

"I hope you don't hog the blankets," she said.

"I hope you don't snore."

Callie chuckled and hit him with one of the bed pillows.

He laughed.

Her eyes were drifting shut as he buried his nose in her hair. Softly, she whispered, "Jammer?"

"Yes?"

"If I didn't have leverage, would I have ended up like Joost and Dieter?"

There was only silence in answer to her question. It spoke volumes.

CALLIE WOKE TO THE MOST delicious scents, her nostrils flaring at the smell of freshly cooked eggs, mushrooms and peppers and the heavenly fragrance of coffee.

"Caffeine," she murmured against the downy softness of the pillow. "This had better not be a dream."

She heard a low chuckle and suddenly realized that she was alone in the big bed.

"Come on, sleepyhead. It's time to rise and shine."

"Just five more minutes, Mom."

He laughed and then said, "I've got omelets and coffee. I even made fresh-squeezed orange juice."

"Okay, then I think I'll keep you around for a decade or so. Gimme."

She emerged from the covers and discovered that he was carrying a tray and had nothing on except an apron tied around his taut middle.

"Eggs and a naked man. What more could I have asked for?"

"How about cream in your coffee?"

"Pour it on, buster, and give me a fork and a napkin. The fork for the eggs and the napkin for my drool."

"At your service."

"You can service me later. I'll eat now."

He set the tray in front of her, and without hesitation, Callie dug in. She groaned at the first bite as she discovered that Jammer had also used a little salsa in the omelet. The combined taste of the peppers, mushrooms and salsa stimulated her taste buds until they were dancing. "Damn, Jammer, your cooking is spoiling me for other men."

He frowned at that. "Then I'd better stop."

"This is the heartiest breakfast I've had in a long time. Are you trying to fatten me up?"

"You're going to need your energy today."

"Why is that? Are we going to spend the day in bed?"

His eyes flared at that, but he smiled and shook his head. "No, it's harvest time. Don't you want to see what we do here?"

"Oh, I'd love to."

"Then finish up and have your shower. I'll go first so I'm not tempted."

He turned and walked away from her, giving her an eyeful of the perfectly muscled globes of his ass. "Nice butt," she said. He threw a look over his shoulder, grinned and shut the bathroom door.

True to his word, Jammer drove her in a small cart down into the vineyards, where the clusters of grapes were heavy on the vine. Many people were already there, easily detaching the fruit with small curved knives.

At least, Callie *thought* it was easy until Jammer put one of those curved knives in her hand and started teaching her the maneuver.

"Leave a little bit of stem on the end, so we can handle the cluster," he said, showing her a whole different side to him. A patient side.

Together, shoulder to shoulder, they harvested all the way down the row.

The sky was beautiful, the air washed clean from the short thunderstorm the night before. The temperature was perfect to be out in her black tank top and white peasant skirt.

As she moved along, she put the grapes in yellow buckets to be picked up by the truck.

"How did you get involved with this vineyard?" she asked, checking to make sure no one was in hearing distance.

"It was a cover, pure and simple, a place for me to escape to when I wasn't traveling. Who would have guessed that I would love it? Jim was great in teaching me what I needed to know. At first he assumed I was one of those corporate types making an investment in a business I was totally ignorant about. I think he was surprised when I caught on and started running it. Then he was worried I would let him go, but of course I need someone here when business calls me away."

He turned to look at her with a perfectly content smile. She brushed a leaf out of his dark hair, returning his smile. She bent back to the vines, trying to decide how big a fool she was for letting herself get caught up in Jammer. Really caught up in him, so that she almost believed in this fairy tale.

She gave herself a reality check. This wasn't going to last. This beautiful place would be seized by the government. Jammer would be tried, convicted and condemned to a very long prison sentence. Callie would go on to the next mission.

She had to keep that firmly planted in her head. She would play her part to the fullest. But standing in the bright sunlight, she dreaded the moment when she would reveal who she was. She dreaded the look in his eyes and the expression on his face from learning he had been so deeply betrayed. She wished she could avoid that, but was too much of a Watchdog agent to let anyone else collar the Ghost.

The grapes were taken to the crush pad and they started to unload them. The physical labor felt good, and Callie was interested in every aspect of the production of wine.

Jim started running the grapes up a conveyor belt that took the clusters into the de-stemmer, a machine that also cut the grapes in half and made pulp out of them. She watched as the grape pulp was pumped into what Jim called a "bladder press" that squeezed out the juice.

By the time this process was complete the sun was dipping in the sky. Callie was sitting on the edge of the loading dock, resting, when Jammer came up to her and said, "Want to help me out?"

"With what?" she asked. His expression was full of mischief.

"A tradition."

"Really? What type of tradition?"

"Stop asking questions and come on."

He slipped his hands around her waist and very slowly let her slide down his body.

"Does this tradition involve something hard?"

"Yes, in a way."

"Lead on."

He brought her around the end of the crush pad to a wooden vat set up next to the building. A short set of stairs was pushed close to it.

She walked up the little flight of steps and looked inside the vat. It was filled with tons of grapes. "You want to what? Crush them?"

"Exactly."

She laughed. Jammer went over to a CD player and pushed a button. Beautiful Italian opera poured from the speakers. Callie laughed again.

"Jim, if you would do the honors."

Jim came over with a bucket and indicated that Callie should remove her sandals and dip her feet into the water. Jim gave them a quick scrub and then it was Jammer's turn.

"Everything's been de-stemmed so you won't hurt your feet," Jammer explained.

Callie stepped down into the vat, finding the grapes warm from the sun's rays. She tucked her skirt into her waistband and started to walk on the grapes.

"Squishy. So this is something you do every year?"

"Yes. Jim says it makes the wine better to have some grapes crushed the old-fashioned way. Who's to argue?"

"It's fun," Callie said as she started to move a little faster, pumping her legs up and down.

Jim poured each of them a glass of wine. Callie sipped and crushed, releasing the juices, the sweet smell of the grapes permeating her senses, heightened by the wine.

Around and around they went, until the grapes beneath their feet turned into pulp. Juice started to fly up as they continued to wade through the mush, the haunting Italian music a perfect backdrop to a perfect day.

At one point, she looked over at Jammer. His clothes were rumpled, his hair a tousled mess, and he had a hint of beard stubble shadowing his jaw. She'd seen him in a suit; she knew how well he cleaned up. But her heart lurched at the carefree look on his face. This was the real man under Jammer's sexy and tough facade.

The real man who turned toward her and got caught by her eyes as if she'd reached out and touched him. She reveled in the knowledge that Jammer couldn't see her without wanting her. An ache spread inside her, a tangible thing that took on a life of its own.

Everything that touched her was warm—the grapes beneath her feet, the waning sun, Jammer's dark eyes. Her breath hitched and stammered in her lungs as he drew close to her. The music swelled into an arching crescendo that brought tears to her eyes.

He captured her face between his palms, his expression mirroring the ache that had spread to every part of her. His eyes locked on to hers so intently it was a physical connection. There was communication between them though neither spoke.

He just held her gaze for the longest moment. Then he took her hand and pulled it up to his mouth. He kissed her wrist and palm.

Then without a word, Jammer led her out of the vat and across the yard into the house, through the back door.

They walked up the stairs to the bedroom. Her heart was pounding so hard she thought she was going to swoon.

He stopped in the doorway and pushed her hair from her face, framing her cheeks with his palms. "You are an amazing woman. All those intriguing layers. Peeling them away every day would be an unending joy for me. Delving into your soul and discovering every inch of who you are, inside and out. I love your confidence and your sense of humor."

"And when that wears off? When it grows old?" she asked.

"Life offers no guarantees. You know that as well as I do. But we are who we are, flawed, tough because we have to be, and doing exactly what our hearts dictate. It's not a matter of getting it out of my system. It's more a matter of integrating it into my life, so I can live that passion every day."

She stared up into his eyes, feeling the force of every word, the complete honesty. But it did them absolutely no good.

Their relationship had been doomed from the very beginning.

She wouldn't be on this mission if she wasn't committed to apprehending criminals and protecting the citizens of the United States.

She'd mistakenly thought this assignment would be a piece of cake.

She'd been so wrong.

Body shaking, lips trembling, she held that intense gaze, held on to it tightly, and smiled. But she didn't get to say anything—his cell rang.

It took Jammer a moment to let go of her, a moment to pull the mantle of the arms dealer back on. The music abruptly ended outside as Jammer put the phone to his ear.

"Fuck!" he said, and closed his eyes.

Callie waited while he conversed, pacing up and

down. When he'd finished he threw the phone. It hit the pillows on the bed.

"What?" she asked softly, gently putting her hand on his arm.

"I think I'm so damn smart. I just shot myself in the foot."

"How?"

"The shipment that Joost and Dieter promised me just got confiscated by the U.S. fucking Navy." He ran his hands through his hair and locked them behind his neck. He leaned against the open bedroom door.

"Oh God. Where?" Callie felt her mission spinning out of control—and taking the Ghost out of her reach. She had evidence of some buys he'd done, but nothing that tied him to selling weapons to a Colombian drug lord, which would seal his fate. She pushed away her soft feelings. Something would have to be done. She was not going to fail in her mission.

"San Diego. Two planes flew my order to a small airport. The cargo was supposed to be combined with my complete shipment and then flown on to Colombia. But SEALs were there training and they entered the wrong plane. My plane. Now the weapons have been moved to the navy base. They'll trace them back to Joost, but not to me. I've conveniently taken out the only man who can supply me with what I need for this deal with Fuentes. Damn, Eduardo is going to be livid. He might even cut me out of the deal. I can't have that."

"Since we can't replace those weapons, then we have only one choice."

Startled, Jammer turned to look at her. "What are you saying?"

"We break into the naval station and steal our weapons back."

11

JAMMER STARED AT GINA for a moment. "Are you serious? A naval base?"

"I have contacts. I can get us in and pilot the plane."

He saw the wheels turning in her head. Of course she would have contacts. Gillian Santiago was a very resourceful woman who had been appointed by the president; if the Watchdog director couldn't pull strings, no one could. "So can I," he said, warming to the idea.

"Then I say we start planning on how we're going to do this. Let me make some phone calls and see what I can find out."

He grabbed her around the waist and kissed her. "Why are you doing this?"

"My cut is tied up in this deal, Jammer. I don't work for nothing."

For the umpteenth time he wondered how deep her feelings for him went. If she was in turmoil about arresting him, she never showed it. But in bed, he knew she wasn't playacting. "Ah, business again."

Her eyes flashed. "That's right. I have to keep my eye on the bottom line. I'm going to shower first because I'm very sticky," Gina said as she ducked into the bathroom.

"I'll start making my own calls." Jammer dialed the director. At least this time he wasn't waking him up. Stanford answered on the first ring. "Yes," he said.

"I have a major problem."

"What is it?"

"My weapons have been seized by the U.S. Navy. I have a warehouse in San Diego housing the bulk of the shipment. All of it is scheduled to be flown out tomorrow. Unfortunately, there was a fluke incident at the airport and SEALs entered my plane instead of the decoy one they were training with. They ended up confiscating both planes."

"Let me do some digging. Sit tight and I will get back to you. I know someone over in the Alcohol, Tobacco and Firearms department. He should be aware of what is happening."

"We can't afford to have this deal go south. We'll lose Fuentes, and three years of hard work will go down the drain."

"We're not going to lose him. I guarantee you that much. I'll do everything in my power to get you access to the base, but you'll have to figure out how to get those weapons out. I can even supply you with some people to help if that's necessary."

"Thank you. That will help."

"And the Watchdog agent?"

"I suspect she's on the phone with her boss right now."

"That's good. We'll both have strings to pull, and

believe me, Gillian has a lot of pull. I'll get back to you before the hour is out."

"I'll be waiting for your phone call."

Gina—aka Callie Carpenter—exited the bathroom looking delectable and smelling delicious.

When Jammer went past her, he gave her a quick kiss on the mouth. He couldn't imagine what she was thinking. She only knew him as an arms dealer. There would come a time when he would reveal to her who he really was and why he had done what he had, but that wasn't now.

She was already turning away and dialing her phone. He went inside the bathroom and took a quick shower, washing off the sticky grape juice and the grime of the day.

After this was all over, he would lose this place that he had called home for three years. Losing Callie would be hard enough. Losing the winery would be almost as difficult. He loved it with a passion.

When the DEA had purchased this property for his cover, Jammer was at first amused. He was told that he could either use it as a base of operations, live there when not on business, or grow grapes and make wine. The last of those choices would solidify his cover.

But now that his cover was blown he had to assume a new identity. When Fuentes found out who the Ghost really was, he would be livid. The man had too much pride not to come after Jammer, whether he was in prison or not. Fuentes would be sure to murder anyone Jammer held dear. That was why he had to disappear—and he had to go alone.

He exited the bathroom, but Callie wasn't in the room. He got dressed and went looking for her.

She was outside, pacing and talking on the phone. So he let her be. When his stomach rumbled, he decided that preparing a meal would be both a stress reliever and alleviate their hunger.

He pulled some ingredients out of the fridge and set them on the counter. He rubbed two bass fillets with olive oil and seasoning, stuffing them with sliced onions and oregano sprigs and tying them with string.

Sliding them into the oven, he moved on to the Mediterranean-inspired salad made up of garlic, anchovy paste, olive oil, grape and cherry tomatoes, Kalamata olives from Spain, sun-dried tomatoes and chopped oregano.

By the time Callie came back into the kitchen, the fish was almost done and the salad was chilling in the fridge.

"Wow, that smells heavenly and I'm starving. What are you making?"

"Roasted black sea bass with tomato and olive salad."

He started to set the table and Callie put down her phone to help.

"How did it go?" Jammer asked.

"I'm getting my gear delivered here in about two hours, and contracted four people to back us up. I also got the base plans and the rotation schedule for the guards. It's best to use a water egress rather than a frontal assault. I've secured boats and scuba equipment," Callie replied, arranging forks and knives.

"You do have yourself some nice contacts."

She shot him a look. "Hey, I'm not just a pretty face."

He chuckled and got a stab of pain thinking that he would never get a chance to find out all he could about Callie Carpenter. It was a complicated mess. Drew Miller was marrying Callie's sister, Allie Carpenter, and he and Miller hadn't parted on the best of terms. The DEA had helped her brother, Max, disappear along with Rio Marshall for their own protection. It was one of the demands he'd put to Stanford in exchange for completing the mission with Fuentes. So now that both of them were out of danger, all he had to do was worry about Callie getting on Fuentes's radar.

He'd done his best in the three years he'd played this low-life arms dealer to keep people out of harm's way and still obtain his objective.

"You sound like you know your way around a military base," Jammer said.

"You could say that. I was a military brat when I was a kid, so I know the ropes," Callie replied.

The oven timer went off. Jammer went over and took out the fish. He set the fillets on plates, then added the salad.

Callie seated herself, and Jammer set her plate down in front of her.

She breathed in the sizzling fish's aroma. As soon as Jammer took a chair and poured the wine, she dug in.

He would never get tired of watching her, especially with that expression of pure rapture on her face.

"Where did you learn to cook this way?" she asked between bites.

Sick of ducking questions and offering half-truths, Jammer said softly, "My mother. She was a master in the kitchen. We ate like this every night."

"That must have been fantastic."

"It was. She was a stay-at-home mom, and all my friends were jealous when I told them that when I got home from school, my mom would have something waiting for me. It was either pizza bagels, hot soup on a cold day or my favorite chocolate-chip cookies still warm from the oven."

He looked up at Callie and she had stopped eating. He knew she realized that he was telling her an actual piece of his life. Just as he had when she'd asked about the book in the library and he'd talked about his father.

He smiled wistfully. "I guess we were spoiled."

"You were blessed," she said. "Truly."

He nodded, his throat tight. It pained him that she would never get a chance to meet his parents and that they wouldn't get the chance to meet her.

He ached that he would have to change his life again, become someone else and sacrifice this woman who meant more to him than any woman had in his life.

She reached over and covered his hand with hers. "I was lucky, too. Very lucky with my parents."

"Are they disappointed in what you do?"

"They don't know what I do, Jammer, and I like it that way. They wouldn't approve, but I have to live my life the way I see fit."

He realized that she wasn't talking about Gina

Callahan, but Callie Carpenter. Of course, being a black ops agent, Callie wouldn't be able to tell her parents what she did for a living.

"What would you do if you could do anything you wanted?"

"I've thought about that often. After all, being an arms dealer is already starting to get old. I think I'd go to law school."

Jammer laughed so hard he choked.

She had to slap him on the back and get him a glass of water.

"I know," she said with amusement in her voice. "It's an odd choice."

He also realized that it was Callie who would become the lawyer, and she'd be a great one. She was smart and thought quickly on her feet.

"Give a guy a warning next time," he said, his voice hoarse from the coughing.

"Sorry." She giggled and took another bite of her meal. Shortly after that, they left their empty plates and drifted out into the night.

"It is simply breathtaking here," she said. She sat down on the edge of the pool and dangled her feet in the water. Jammer settled behind her and did the same.

He wrapped his arms around her, and she sighed wistfully. "Have you thought about what you will do after this deal with Fuentes is done?"

"Do more deals," he lied.

"Why? I mean, you must have amassed a fortune, and arms dealing is such a risky and dangerous profession.

It would be smart to get out. I can tell how much you love this place. Why not make wine?"

"I'll think about it," he said. The fact that she was so intuitive about him made him both happy and sad. He wasn't going to be able to stay here once Fuentes was arrested.

He kissed the nape of her neck. She sighed and leaned her head back, resting it on his shoulder.

It gave him better access to her throat. He slid his lips along the column and sucked her earlobe into his mouth. She shivered in his arms and twisted her head, presenting her mouth to him for a kiss.

"Hey, you two lovebirds. We've got work to do."

A heavy bag dropped on the pool deck. Callie and Jammer turned to find Drew Miller and three other men standing behind them—one Asian, one blond and a man with dark hair drawn into a ponytail.

Callie got up and rounded on the newcomers. "Drew! How many times have I told you not to sneak up on me?"

Miller glanced at Callie for only a brief moment. Without broadcasting his intentions, he walked up to Jammer and socked him in the jaw. Coldcocked, Jammer took the blow that drove him back and into the pool.

When he surfaced, he could hear Callie cursing the man out, but Jammer calmly walked up the stairs and faced Miller.

"Jammer—" she said, glaring at Drew.

Jammer held up his hand. "No, I deserved that."

"You're a slick bastard, Jammer. I'll give you that.

But I owed that to you for Tina," Drew said, his eyes narrow and filled with vindication.

"I get it."

Drew did quick introductions. "This is Kyoto, Michaels and Frost. Well, let's get going. We only have a few hours to get this show on the road. Midnight is the bewitching hour, my friends," Drew said, picking up the black bag and looking at Callie. "The gear you wanted is in here."

They went into the kitchen and cleared off the table. Drew pulled out the map of the base.

"The front part of the facility is heavily guarded, but the approach to the airstrip isn't as bad and the guard rotation changes at twelve midnight. It's the best time to infiltrate the base and hijack the airplanes. Do you need me to fly shotgun, Gina?"

"Yes," she said. "The rest of you hightail it out of there once we rev up those engines."

The three men nodded.

Just then the doorbell rang and four more steely eyed men dressed in black entered Jammer's residence—courtesy of Director Stanford.

Jammer made the introductions and said, "Gear up. Let's take our merchandise back."

CALLIE SAT NEXT TO JAMMER in the black SUV as they rode to the water, where they would switch to boats. She already had her scuba gear on. She'd memorized the map and was thankful that Gillian had pinpointed exactly what hangars the planes were in, as well as the type of plane.

Callie could fly just about anything, but it was nice to know in advance what she was up against.

She glanced over at Drew, who was driving. He was an extremely capable agent, but a bit of a rogue. When he had hit Jammer, she thought she was going to faint. But Jammer had taken it, and he had the bruise darkening his jaw to show for it.

She was being a fool. She *knew* that, but she still reached up and ran the back of her fingers along the swelling. Jammer turned his head slightly to acknowledge her caress.

She dropped her hand and tensed as they approached the area. It didn't take long to inflate the boats and speed to the point where they had to go into the water.

They swam around all the obstacles until they were able to make landfall. Once they hit the beach, all scuba gear was discarded and one of the men bundled it up and swam back out.

Drew automatically took point, heading for the hangars dead ahead. He whispered, "Watch out for guards. They should be thin, but it's best not to take any chances." With hand gestures, he made his intent well known: move forward.

They stayed low, and Callie was happy to see that clouds had obscured the moon as they made their way up to the gargantuan hangars. Frost did his magic to disable security, and they all ducked in.

The cargo planes were sitting side by side in the hangar. Callie started to move toward one, but Jammer grabbed her arm and pulled her to him. He kissed her soundly and then let her go.

"Be careful."

"I will. You, too."

"I'll see you both in Colombia."

Drew nodded and whispered to Kyoto, "Find the controls and get those doors open as fast as you can. Let's get these birds ready for takeoff."

Jammer jerked his head at one of his men and Callie watched as they disappeared into one of the planes. Callie and Drew entered the other.

Settling herself in the pilot's seat, she went through a preflight check very quickly. Just as they started the engines, the doors to the hangar opened.

"Here we go," Drew said softly.

As soon as the engine was ready, Callie eased the plane out of the hangar and wasted no time pointing its nose toward the runway, her mind on takeoff.

Just then alarms sounded, and men came running. She saw Kyoto, Frost and Michaels put their hands up.

"They're great at playacting, aren't they?" Drew said as they gunned the engine and took off into the sky.

She could only hope that Jammer was close behind her. It wasn't long before his voice came over the radio and she knew they were free and clear.

"This was all a ruse to fool Jammer?" asked Callie, making sure their radios were off so Jammer couldn't hear the conversation.

"Yeah, the base commander took care of the details and our guys were released as soon as the planes were safely in the air."

"Wow, that took some pull."

"Gillian has it, my friend. She went straight to the president."

"All I care about is that these weapons will soon be in Colombia and this deal with Fuentes will happen. We can move in on the Ghost once the DEA gets the leaders of the Libertad."

"Yeah, Gillian wants me to rendezvous with the head DEA agent in Colombia once we get there. Will you be all right alone with this guy, Callie?"

"I can handle the Ghost," Callie said, trying to keep her tone neutral.

"Yeah. Isn't that a kick in the pants? He was right under our noses the whole time."

"You have to admire that, though. He hid in plain sight."

"Didn't say I didn't admire it, but how are *you* doing with keeping your feelings for him compartmentalized?"

So much for neutral. She sighed. "As best I can. I won't lie to you, Drew. He's a lot different from the man I thought he was."

"That's the trouble with working undercover. Nothing's black and white. I've liked quite a few guys I've had to take down. Didn't make it easier, but I didn't hesitate," Drew said.

"I won't, either. I promise."

"I know you won't. You're Allie's sister."

THE FLIGHT TO CARTAGENA took approximately six hours. As soon as they reached Colombian airspace, they were directed to a place to land. Once the planes were on the ground, Drew and Callie disembarked to greet a large number of men who were there to unload the weapons for delivery to Fuentes.

Drew took his leave and made his way toward the city. Callie and Jammer got into the waiting black SUV and were soon at Fuentes's compound.

The house was beautiful, with white stucco walls and numerous plants and trees giving it a lush, tropical look. They were ushered up the stairs and into the residence.

Fuentes was there to meet them at the door. He shook hands with Jammer, then ogled Callie.

First his eyes narrowed and he took his time with her face, his eyes touching on her hair, then traveling down her body. They lingered on her breasts before he finished his slow exploration.

Callie did not like the look in his eyes and wanted to do the man bodily harm.

Jammer didn't move, in fact he didn't seem to pay her any attention. It surprised her, because he'd been so protective of her until now. Then it dawned on her. He didn't want Fuentes to know that he cared.

"A very beautiful woman. Perhaps we can do some deals of our own," he said suggestively.

Jammer walked into the house while Fuentes crowded her. She forced a smile. "As long as your money is green, *señor,* I think that will be quite possible."

Very deftly she sidestepped him and his outstretched hand, and he returned to business, addressing both of them as he followed Jammer inside.

"First, I must insist that all weapons be turned over

to my guards. Your room has been readied. Please enjoy some refreshments. Since you are a day early, we will have some time to get acquainted," Fuentes said, his eyes on Callie. "I took the liberty of providing some garments for you both, as I understood you had to travel light. Please make yourselves at home. I must leave you now to take care of some pressing business. Jammer, please accompany me."

As they left the room, a woman approached her. When Callie looked up, she met the eyes of Leila Mendez, a Watchdog operative. She was dressed as a maid and offered Callie food from a tray.

"What can I get you to drink?" she asked in accented English.

Callie shook her head and acknowledged Leila with a nod.

Leila suddenly dropped the tray, and while the guards in the room were distracted, slipped Callie a note. In Spanish, she apologized profusely, and after cleaning up the mess, she left.

"I think I'll retire now," Callie told the guards. "Please lead the way to my accommodations."

One guard escorted her down a hall and opened one of the doors. Callie went inside the room and closed it behind her. She sat down on the bed and opened the note.

"Meet me on the balcony."

As she watched, the ink disappeared from the paper. Callie discarded it in a wastebasket.

She went to the French doors and opened them, stepping out. Leila rapelled down from an upstairs balcony, landing silently.

"Gillian sends her congratulations for a job well done. That plane heist went off without a hitch."

Callie nodded.

"The buy goes down tomorrow. The DEA and government forces are amassing a few miles from town. These are the coordinates in case you need to get out of here in a hurry, and here is a gun. I'm sure the guards took yours. Once the buy is done, the undercover agent will reveal himself and that will spring the trap. So keep your head down and your eyes on the Ghost. If I know that guy, he will have a contingency plan."

"Agreed," Callie said, realizing that this would be her last night with Jammer.

"THAT IS A SPECIAL WOMAN," Fuentes said as the door closed behind them. He moved behind a large desk. He opened an intricately scrolled box and took out a cigar, neatly clipped the end and lit it. Taking a puff, he grinned.

Jammer wished he could wipe the smirk off Fuentes's face with his fist. It took all his willpower not to react. "She's quite a spitfire and keeps me on my toes. But we don't need to talk about her. We have more pressing matters to discuss."

"Indeed, we do. The Ghost will be here when?"

"Tomorrow, exactly as I promised. Is everything set?"

"Yes, yes. Everything is ready at my end. It is fortuitous that you were able to secure my shipment. The consequences of your failure would have been severe. I'm afraid that your boss, the Ghost, would have lost his right-hand man."

"Then it's a good thing that I'm resourceful."

"Yes, it is. I have heard quite a bit about your friend Gina Callahan. She has quite a reputation. Is all of it true?"

"All that and more."

"That is good. It is satisfying to spar with a woman with spunk, makes the taming of her all the better. Don't you agree?"

Jammer clenched his fist behind his back, tamping down his need to protect Callie. Fuentes would learn soon enough what it meant to fuck with the United States in general and the DEA in particular.

He used the memory of his dead colleagues to keep himself in check. This wasn't about him or Callie. It was about them, and he would see that justice was served. He would put Fuentes behind bars and make sure it was his testimony that kept him there.

Fuentes indicated that Jammer should sit down. From a crystal decanter, he poured out a snifter of brandy for each of them.

Jammer forced himself to move, shoving the tension out of his body. He reached for the glass and settled into the chair.

"I haven't made any progress in finding that bitch of a DEA agent and her bodyguard. She had the gall to spy on my compound and the nerve to escape me before I was finished with her. Damn DEA, they will never learn. I kill their agents as fast as they send them."

"So she's the one that got away, eh?"

"Yes, she made a mockery of me and that I cannot tolerate. After this deal is complete, I want you to find them for me. When you do, I want them eliminated and I want them to suffer. You will do this for me?"

"Eduardo, the Ghost keeps me busy with other jobs."

"But murder is something you've done in the past. You surely do as the Ghost tells you."

"I am at his service."

"I will speak with him tomorrow. If he orders you to, then will you kill them?"

"I will complete whatever task the Ghost puts in front of me, Eduardo."

The man nodded and slammed away from his desk. "I can't believe that little bitch got away from me twice. In the meantime, I've had to keep my guard up. A smashed phone was found near where she was held captive. I fear that there may be a traitor in my compound."

"We'll have to ferret him out," Jammer said with a slight smile, thinking that the phone he'd left had effectively made Eduardo paranoid. Taken the focus off Rio and Max.

"Yes, and when we do, I'll cut his heart out."

"Sounds like a fitting end for a traitor."

"It is."

"I will say *buenos noches,* Eduardo."

Jammer rose and set the snifter of brandy on the edge of the desk, then walked to the door. He reached for the handle just as Eduardo said, "I will have your woman."

12

JAMMER WENT RED-HOT inside. He almost lost control and leaped across the desk to pummel Fuentes. But he tamped the urge down. Eduardo wouldn't ever touch Callie.

"You are welcome to her," Jammer said, "once this buy is over and I am done with her."

Eduardo chuckled. "I now have even more to look forward to."

Jammer made sure that he shut the door in an easy and controlled way. He stalked down the hall and met up with a guard, who took him to his room.

He went inside, but Callie wasn't there. Then he saw the open French doors and thought he caught voices. He made his way to the balcony, where he found her.

Callie turned. "Oh, hi. I didn't hear you come in."

Jammer looked around. "Were you talking to someone out here?"

"No. How did it go?"

"Eduardo wants to make you his love slave."

"Like hell he does. He even tries and I'll make him a soprano. Then I'll really get mean."

Jammer chuckled, releasing the last of the tension in his body. He pulled her to him and wrapped his arms around her to hold her tight. She slipped her arms around his neck. "Everything will work out just fine," Jammer said into her sweet-smelling hair.

Deep down he knew that it wouldn't be fine. He would nab Fuentes and Callie would go back to Watchdog with the satisfaction that she had helped put away a dangerous and ruthless drug lord. But the fact that they couldn't be together weighed heavily on him. He knew it had to be done, but every time he tried to put distance between them, they became closer than ever.

"Your indifference out there when Fuentes was ogling me... That was an act, right?"

He hugged her tighter. "Of course. I don't want him to sense how much you mean to me."

"I knew that, but I just needed to hear you say it."

He let her go and met her eyes. "I'm the one who said you shouldn't be here. You remember that? I wanted you as far away from Fuentes as you could get, but circumstances dictated that I bring you along."

"Yes, I remember, and now I see why, but I had to be here. I had to see it through."

"I know why you had to come." He knew her dedication to her job and the need to carry out her goal of arresting the Ghost and bringing him to justice were all that mattered. He also knew that she was torn by the discovery. He liked to think it was because she cared for him on a deeper level. But he wasn't going to be a fool. She'd never shown any indication that she cared for him.

"We'd better get some sleep. We'll need to be fresh for tomorrow when the buy goes down."

"All right," she said, her eyes dark with her own secrets and her own agenda.

He went inside, but Callie didn't immediately follow. He turned to find her watching him. Her eyes went over every inch of him, from his hair down to his feet.

"Jammer, this is our last night together, isn't it? Tomorrow will change everything."

"Don't…don't talk about it."

"It will change, and we can't get away from it no matter how much we want to." She said it quietly and, if he wasn't mistaken, with real regret.

"No, I guess we can't."

She reached over and picked an exotic flower off a vine growing close to the house. She came into the room but left the French doors open. Dimming the lights, she walked up to Jammer and slipped her hands under his shirt. Her palms were cool, and the petals of the flower whispered over his skin like butterfly wings. He shuddered as she lifted off his shirt.

She slid her hands up over his pectoral muscles and back down to his waistband, unbuckling, unbuttoning and unzipping.

With her palm in the middle of his chest, she pushed him onto the chaise longue.

"You look like a Greek god lying there."

"I'm just a flesh-and-blood man and I need you."

"I need you, too. I need you so much."

She leaned across him, still fully clothed. As she began to kiss his chest, he started to undress her. When she opened her mouth over his flat nipple, he moaned and jerked her toward him. She gasped and he rid her of the rest of her clothes.

She kissed him then and her mouth was warm and soft against his. He poured himself into the kiss, knowing that their time grew short. His hands found her breasts and he cupped them, rubbing his palms over her engorged nipples, jerking her up until he could suck first one, then the other into his mouth. She cried out softly, lowered herself farther and farther down his body until she took him into her mouth.

His hips bucked and he moaned at the hot contact, at the tingling, sleek strokes of her tongue as she pulled at him.

It was difficult not to be restless, not to move his body, shift his limbs, in an effort to ease the ache that her expert mouth created in his every muscle and pore. He twisted on the chaise, his hips thrusting uncontrollably. Breaking her contact, he yanked her up against him and pushed into her so hard she cried out and climaxed. He grunted as she took him, held him, moved over him, matching him stroke for stroke as she continued to pulsate and shudder around him. He had no recourse, no way to stop the climax rushing to overtake him, and didn't even try. She grasped his biceps, arching back as he came with a long, jerking groan. It was as if he couldn't get deep enough, couldn't pour enough of himself into her. It was beyond seeking physical pleasure. It was as if his soul recognized her and only her.

They clasped each other when it was over, and his voice was hoarse when he said, "How am I going to let you go?"

She pressed her face against his neck and said softly, "Don't let me go right now. Don't let go."

He held on tightly to her, shifting them to the bed, where they curled into each other.

He didn't want to sleep. He wanted to hold her for as long as he could. But when sleep came, his arms didn't loosen around her.

THE COOL BREEZE on her skin woke her as she shifted on the mattress to glance at the clock. Still early. She snuggled up to Jammer, then felt her stomach lurch. Today would be the day she arrested him for crimes against the U.S. It was going to hurt very badly.

She rolled away from him and got up to take a shower. Under the spray, she hardened herself; she could have no mercy. She would have to treat him like any other criminal. Detaching herself wasn't going to be easy, but she had to do it. Powerful emotions twisted in her chest but she shoved them down. The time had come for her to fulfill her mission.

When she came out of the bathroom, Jammer smiled at her and went in. When he was done, they went for breakfast.

Fuentes was in the dining room and it wasn't long before they were served eggs, bacon and fruit. Someone brought Callie coffee and juice. She ate, keeping her eyes on her plate and away from what she was sure were lecherous looks from the drug lord.

Jammer conversed with him in a monotone voice. When breakfast was done, Fuentes pushed back from the table. The sound of trucks filtered through the open windows. Fuentes checked his watch and smiled. "Ah, our guests are arriving. It's time to seal the deal with the Libertad."

"Gina, I was wondering if I could talk to you for a moment up in the room?" Jammer said.

Callie looked at him, then at Fuentes. The smug smile that crawled across the man's face made her skin crawl. "Sure," she said with a smile of her own, as if she wasn't aware that Fuentes intended to make her his. Not damned likely.

She followed Jammer back to the bedroom. He closed the door behind her, took her hand and brought her over to a chair in the corner. It had heavy metal sides and weighed a ton, but was very comfortable.

"Have a seat," he said. When she did, she was too slow to stop the slide and click of the handcuffs that encircled her wrist. When she pulled, she found herself shackled to the chair.

"What the..." she said, looking down at the cuffs, then up at Jammer.

He backed away and grabbed the bag he'd brought with him to Colombia.

"I'm sorry, Callie."

She jerked her head upright at the sound of her name—her real name—on his lips. Fear twisted through her, that she might finally be at the mercy of Jammer. This time he knew she had every intention of betraying him.

"You know who I am?"

"I always have. From the very beginning, I knew everything."

"How is that possible?"

He turned around and slipped a gun into his waistband at the small of his back.

"You have someone on the inside," she said.

"You could say that."

Suddenly she realized who he was—the undercover DEA agent! "All this time I've been chasing you and you've been on our side all along. Three years of my life have just been rendered meaningless."

"No, they haven't, Callie. You and the other agencies protected my every step."

"How do you figure that?"

"You built my cover by making me notorious. It brought me to the attention of Fuentes—my ultimate goal. So nothing you did was meaningless. Every action was a stepping-stone to justice."

She couldn't argue with his logic, and it did give her satisfaction that she had helped to keep this man safe. "Gillian's going to be so pissed."

"I'm sure a lot of government agencies will." He came back over to the chair. "It has to be this way. I can't be distracted. Do you understand?"

"No. I'm a black ops government agent. I can help you. Now uncuff me!" Relief gave way to anger that Jammer would leave her here in the room while he went out into serious danger.

He shook his head and headed for the door. Callie called to him in the only name she knew. "Jammer!"

He spun around and came back to the chair. He knelt in front of her, his face twisted with emotion. "For once, just this once, I want you to call me by my real name."

Her heart pounded in her chest. "What is your real name?"

She watched him blink quickly, as if he was afraid to take his eyes off her for even a fraction of a second. "It's Shane, Callie. Shane McMasters."

"Shane McMasters is dead," she said bluntly, as if he was playing her. But then she saw the truth in his eyes. He drifted away from her in body and mind, losing himself in a past that haunted his eyes, even now.

"I was. I was a ghost until you opened that hotel room door in Paris. Then I started to live again. I became whole again."

All the emotion she'd contained in her burst free. "Let me go. Don't go out there by yourself. Shane, please don't do this."

"I have to! For my fellow agents who were ambushed by that butcher. He left us for dead. Now he's going to answer for those murders and all his other crimes."

Callie just stared at him, at the wild gleam of pain in his eyes, the muscles and tendons that stood out in his neck, the heavy rise and fall of his chest as he breathed.

He took a badge out of the bag and rubbed the DEA letters with his thumb. When he looked up at her, tears glistened in his eyes. They slipped down his cheeks. She reached out and cupped his jaw. He pressed his forehead to hers. The tears she'd been holding back for so long spilled over and down her own cheeks, mingling with his.

His hand closed around her wrist, as if she was his only anchor. "I love you, Callie."

A sob caught in her throat, his admission slamming into her with actual force. "Oh God, Shane. I love you, too. So don't do this to me. Don't make me wait here not knowing, not being able to help the man I love. I'll never forgive you for this."

Through her tears she watched him struggle with her words.

"I know, but you'll be alive," he said.

He pulled out of her embrace, even as she tried to hold on, to get through to him.

"I've got to go."

"You'll come back to get me. Say that you will."

"I won't. Someone will come to release you. I promise that. But we can't be together."

"Why not?"

"During the trial I'll be in protective custody. After that, I have to disappear. Fuentes won't rest until he finds me, kills me and everyone I love."

"I'll come with you."

"And give up your family? Everyone and everything you know?" Anguish laced his voice. "No. I can't ask that of you. I had to do it and it rips my heart out to know that my sister, Rio, thinks I've been dead for three years."

"No," Callie said softly, but the thought of leaving her family—Allie and Max and her parents—was unbearable. But never to see Jam…Shane again was crushing her heart.

"I love you so much, Callie."

"Shane, no, please don't leave. Please uncuff me."

But he turned, set what looked like the cuff key on the nightstand and walked out of the room. Callie sat there in silence as his footsteps retreated down the hall. Her heart was breaking into little pieces. If anything happened to him, how could she go on? Now that he had revealed his true identity, now that they could really be together, the promise of spending a lifetime with him was something she wanted more than anything.

She pulled at the cuff frantically. Got up and tried to drag the chair, but it wouldn't budge. Then she heard the doorknob turning and she stiffened. If that was him coming back, she was going to kick his ass.

But Leila slipped inside and rushed over to her. "I wondered what happened to you. Did he leave you here for that bastard Fuentes?"

"No, he's undercover DEA."

"What? *He's* the undercover DEA agent we've heard so much about? Those bastards. Trying to get all the glory for themselves. Well, we're not standing for that."

"He left the key on the nightstand," Callie said urgently.

Leila rushed over to the stand and grabbed the key, unlocking the cuffs.

As soon as Callie was free, she went for the gun she'd concealed in her bag. Cocking it and chambering a bullet, she said, "Let's go."

They rushed out the door and down the hall. "This way," Leila said.

Callie followed her through the dining room and into the kitchen. They slipped out the back door and saw Fuentes and several men in green uniforms near an open box of the surface-to-air missiles that Callie had flown to Colombia.

They were laughing and talking like old friends. Shane was walking toward them. Several men with automatic weapons milled about, looking bored.

Callie took a moment to really study the area. She caught glimpses of men in the jungle, but only because she was searching for them.

"The cavalry is here," Leila said softly, "Don't worry."

They moved around the house, and managed to slip up behind the leaders without being detected by using one of the vehicles as cover.

"Ah, here is the Ghost's man. When will your boss be here?" he asked jovially.

"Eduardo, he's already here."

Eduardo looked around. "But I do not see him, *señor*. Is this some kind of joke?"

"No, it's no joke. I'm the Ghost."

"You? What is this!"

"I've used the Ghost as a cover for three years, building my reputation, garnering your interest solely for the purpose of providing this large shipment for you."

"Because you want to work for me?"

Shane laughed and Callie's heart constricted. God, she loved him.

"No. I don't want work for you, you fuck. My real name is Shane McMasters. You left me and five dead DEA agents to rot in the jungle."

"You're DEA! You son of a bitch! It is *you* who are the traitor."

Just then, men came pouring out of the jungle, bristling with weapons. They were dressed in dark jackets with *DEA* printed in white letters on the back. They shouted for everyone to stay where they were. They were accompanied by men dressed in olive drab, toting high-powered weapons.

Fuentes turned and fled. But Shane went after him and tackled him to the ground. Unfortunately, several men pointed their guns at him. Callie aimed carefully. She and Leila opened fire.

With bullets flying, Shane held on to Fuentes and dragged him behind one of the buildings, where Callie lost sight of him. She bolted around the truck, only to come face-to-face with one of the Libertad. She never hesitated. She grabbed his rifle and slammed him in the face with it, at the same time sweeping his feet out from under him. As he went down, she used the butt of the rifle to sock him in the jaw.

He went out like a light. She dropped the rifle and sprinted after Shane and Fuentes. Gunfire cut across her path and she and Leila dived for cover behind another truck.

It looked as if the DEA and the government soldiers had Fuentes's men and the Libertad on the run. Several of their leaders were either putting their hands up or were already dead.

But there was a pocket of resistance still left. She and Leila skirted that group and came around the building. Fuentes had escaped and hidden behind three of his guards, who were effectively pinning Shane down.

"I'll make my way around and we'll come at them from the side and front. I hope you're a good shot," Callie murmured.

"They don't call me dead-eye for nothing," Leila said.

Callie took off and, crouching low, got into position. Then she stood and started shooting to draw their attention away from Shane. That's when Leila took her own shots, dropping all three guards in succession. Fuentes ran for his garage.

"He's heading for his all-terrain," Shane yelled, and started after him.

Leila got sidetracked by a guard. "Keep going," she urged. Callie followed Shane. He reached the garage before she did, and she drew up short when she got inside.

Shane and Fuentes were already duking it out, and Fuentes was losing. Soon he was down, but Shane wouldn't stop. Callie ran over and tugged on his arm, shouting at him that it was enough.

Finally he stopped, dropping back against one of the mammoth wheels of the vehicle Fuentes had been trying to access. Shane's knuckles were bloody as he sat there, breathing heavily, trying to gain his composure.

"It's over," she said. "It's finally over."

"It'll never be over," Shane stated, looking up at her, his eyes filled with raw pain.

"We can make it work."

He shook his head.

Suddenly they were overrun by DEA agents. One of them grabbed Shane's arm and escorted him out. "Wait," Callie said.

Another agent blocked her way. "Just who are you?"

Callie watched as Shane was put into a car and driven away. Fuentes was picked up and also taken. She shoved her way past the DEA agent and met up with Leila—and with Drew.

Her heart felt empty, completely and totally empty. Shane was gone and she was never going to see him again.

IT HAD BEEN THREE WEEKS. Three weeks since Fuentes had been arrested. She'd cried more in that time than she had in her whole life. But Callie had to pick up the pieces and go on. She lounged by a pool in a hotel in Milan, waiting for Reggie to show up with some information she needed.

"Hiya, love."

She looked up to find the Brit in swim trunks that would make a stripper blush. His skin was a deep golden-brown and his blond hair spiked—just like Jammer used to wear his hair. She felt her heart tighten, and was thankful for the sunglasses that hid her eyes.

"Hi, Reggie."

He sat down in the chaise longue next to her and ordered a mai tai. He slid his hand down her sleek leg and smiled at her. "So, what do you say to hooking up? Me and you been dancing around it for some time."

"No, Reggie. I don't think so."

"Ah, still pining for that bloke?"

"Black operatives don't pine. Just give me the information and I'll be on my way."

Reggie smiled and gave her what she needed to know. She closed her eyes and settled back in the chair. "Thanks, Reggie. See you around."

"You bet, love."

She wrapped up the rest of the mission and jumped a plane to D.C., to her apartment. Once home, she listlessly went through her mail, still hoping, still waiting for something from Shane. But there was nothing.

She flipped on the TV to the news and popped some popcorn. Settling down, she was just about to turn the channel when the anchor came on and said, "This is a breaking story. While being transferred today to a more secure facility by the DEA, Eduardo Fuentes was killed when an attempt to free him failed. The attack also left one agent dead, as well as his would-be rescuers."

Callie sat up straighter. The information seeped in. Fuentes was dead. That meant… She could barely let herself even hope. That meant Shane was free to come back to her.

But her hope turned to disappointment when after three days she'd still heard nothing from Shane.

The morning of the fourth day, her doorbell rang and her heart jumped. She ran to answer it, but found it was only a deliveryman.

He handed her a box and had her sign the delivery

slip. Shutting the door, she took the package inside and set it on her table. With her breath suspended in her lungs, she opened the box. Inside was nestled a bottle of Shane's Craving Cherry brandy.

There was no note, no instructions, no greetings. Just the bottle. She remembered that day when they had tasted the cherries. It took her only a moment to make up her mind as to what she was going to do.

SHANE STOOD ON THE PATIO and watched the sun set on the vineyard. His vineyard. The DEA director had accepted his resignation. After Fuentes had died, there was no more reason for him to hide. No more reason for him to be anyone other than who he was.

The DEA had also been generous. Shane had been allowed to keep the vineyard and all the profits it had made as compensation for giving up three years of his life and allowing his sister, Rio, to suffer through his death. He'd even received a special commendation from the president.

He was free and clear and able to do exactly what he wanted for the first time in his life. He was missing only one thing now, one truly colossal and important thing.

"Hey, I have this bottle of cherry brandy and no one to drink it with."

At the sound of her wonderful voice, his whole body stilled, even his heart.

He turned around to find Callie silhouetted against the night, bathed in the light from the kitchen like an angel.

His angel.

"I hear it's quite good," she said softly, her voice breaking.

She set the bottle down on the kitchen table. He wasn't sure how he got to her. Only that he was in her arms as they both dissolved to the patio floor from the sheer emotion of seeing each other again.

They spoke between kisses.

"I waited for you...."

"Wasn't sure you wanted to see me..."

"I love you...Shane."

"It'll take a while getting used to my real name, but now we'll have the time and the freedom to explore each other to the fullest. I love you, Callie."

"Then everything else can be worked out."

Epilogue

"THEY'RE HERE," Callie said as she put the finishing touches on the hors d'oeuvres. Shane was teaching her to cook and it was quite wonderful to discover other pleasures of the body besides what she and Shane did in the bedroom.

"I think I might need a bulletproof vest. The last time your brother-in-law met me he clocked me but good."

"I think you should let me do the talking."

Callie walked to the front door with Shane at her side. When she opened the door, Allie and Drew stood there.

"Hi, sis," her twin said as she embraced Callie. Then she looked at Shane. "Is it true, you are really a DEA agent?"

Shane took Allie's hand in his. "It's true. I'm sorry for what I put you and Drew through when we met. It was part of my job to stay deep undercover."

"You protected us and you destroyed the man who tried to kill my sister. I have no complaints." She reached up and embraced him, giving him a kiss on the cheek.

"Well, *I'm* not going to kiss his cheek," Drew said, then stuck out his hand. "But I'm not going to sock you, either. Welcome to this crazy family." He broke out in a fit of laughter.

Allie, looking perplexed, slapped him on the back. "What's so funny?" she asked as Callie ushered them both into the house.

"Wait until Max finds out. He thought it was bad enough having a black ops guy in the family. Now we have the notorious Ghost."

"See?" Shane said. "I told you I need a bulletproof vest."

"Oh, stop it," Callie retorted, biting her bottom lip. Her brother had better not be difficult.

They were each enjoying a glass of wine and hors d'oeuvres on the patio when the doorbell rang again.

Shane stiffened. "How am I going to face her?"

Callie cupped his face and met his eyes. "She's going to be so happy to see you. You're alive, that's all that's going to matter to her. Now let's go."

This time Shane opened the door. A beautiful, tanned woman stood there with Callie's tall, dark and handsome brother, Max, who was also very tanned.

"Oh God, Shane." Tears gathered, spilled over and ran down her cheeks. "It's really you. They told me everything, but I could scarcely believe it." She wrapped her arms around him and held him tightly. "I missed you so much. I'm so happy to have you back."

"You aren't mad about what I had to do? Pretending to be dead?"

"No. I came to the conclusion that it was you I saw

in that compound. I didn't know why you were there. I was after Fuentes myself and dragged Max into it. I wasn't going to let the man who murdered my brother get away with it. I just knew that it was you I had seen, but that bastard Stanford lied to my face. Though I understand why he did it. It was to protect you. Oh God, I'm babbling. Let me introduce you to Max."

Without a word Max walked up to Shane and punched him in the jaw. Shane stumbled back as Callie and Rio yelled in unison, "Max."

Once again Shane held up his hand. "No. I deserved that, too. Have it out of your system now, Carpenter?"

Max extended his hand just as Drew came into the room, saying, "Dammit, Allie, we missed it."

"Well, you were the one who kissed me first, Drew."

Callie felt tears build in her eyes as Shane shook her brother's hand.

"I also have to thank you for keeping the three women I love more than my own life as safe as you could manage," Max mumbled. "I cannot believe you were a DEA agent on our side the whole time."

Drew laughed and slapped Max on the back. "We're just one happy undercover family."

Shane nodded. He turned to Callie. "There's no need for secrets anymore. Callie, I love you more than anything in this world. Will you marry me?"

She stood there stunned. "Yes," she said. "Yes!" she repeated, and threw herself into his arms.

They stared into each other's eyes as Drew, Allie, Max and Rio drifted away.

"I loved you the moment I saw you in your crazy Gina Callahan persona, but I always knew who you were beneath."

"It was deliciously dangerous to love a man on the wrong side of the law, but I'm so happy with the way things turned out. I'm leaving Watchdog to become a lawyer."

"Watch out, criminal justice system!" He laughed as he pulled her against him, and they walked back to the patio and their family.

* * * * *

*Harlequin Intrigue top author Delores Fossen
presents a brand-new series of breathtaking
romantic suspense!*
TEXAS MATERNITY: HOSTAGES
The first installment available May 2010:
THE BABY'S GUARDIAN

Shaw cursed and hooked his arm around Sabrina.

Despite the urgency that the deadly gunfire created, he tried to be careful with her, and he took the brunt of the fall when he pulled her to the ground. His shoulder hit hard, but he held on tight to his gun so that it wouldn't be jarred from his hand.

Shaw didn't stop there. He crawled over Sabrina, sheltering her pregnant belly with his body, and he came up ready to return fire.

This was obviously a situation he'd wanted to avoid at all cost. He didn't want his baby in the middle of a fight with these armed fugitives, but when they fired that shot, they'd left him no choice. Now, the trick was to get Sabrina safely out of there.

"Get down," someone on the SWAT team yelled from the roof of the adjacent building.

Shaw did. He dropped lower, covering Sabrina as best he could.

There was another shot, but this one came from a rifleman on the SWAT team. Shaw didn't look up, but he heard the sound of glass being blown apart.

The shots continued, all coming from his men, which

meant it might be time to try to get Sabrina to better cover. Shaw glanced at the front of the building.

So that Sabrina's pregnant belly wouldn't be smashed against the ground, Shaw eased off her and moved her to a sitting position so that her back was against the brick wall. They were close. Too close. And face-to-face.

He found himself staring right into those sea-green eyes.

How will Shaw get Sabrina out?
Follow the daring rescue and the heartbreaking
aftermath in THE BABY'S GUARDIAN
by Delores Fossen,
available May 2010 from Harlequin Intrigue.

HARLEQUIN® *Blaze*™

is proud to present

New York Times bestselling author

Vicki Lewis Thompson

with a brand-new trilogy,
SONS OF CHANCE
where three sexy brothers
meet three irresistible women.

Look for the first book
WANTED!

*Available beginning in June 2010
wherever books are sold.*

---

red-hot reads

www.eHarlequin.com

Bestselling Harlequin Presents® author

Lynne Graham

introduces

VIRGIN ON HER WEDDING NIGHT

Valente Lorenzatto never forgave Caroline Hales's
abandonment of him at the altar. But now he's
made millions and claimed his aristocratic Venetian
birthright—and he's poised to get his revenge.
He'll ruin Caroline's family by buying out their
company and throwing them out of their mansion...
unless she agrees to give him the wedding night
she denied him five years ago....

**Available May 2010
from Harlequin Presents!**

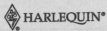

INTRIGUE

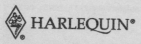

HARLEQUIN®

American ★ Romance®

LAURA MARIE ALTOM

The Baby Twins

Stephanie Olmstead has her hands full raising
her twin baby girls on her own. When she runs
into old friend Brady Flynn, she's shocked to find
herself suddenly attracted to the handsome airline
pilot! Will this flyboy be the perfect daddy—
or will he crash and burn?

Babies
&
Bachelors
USA

"LOVE, HOME & HAPPINESS"

www.eHarlequin.com

HAR75309

Former bad boy Sloan Hawkins is back in Redemption, Oklahoma, to help keep his aunt's cherished garden thriving and to reconnect with the girl he left behind, Annie Markham. But when he discovers his secret child—and that single mother Annie never stopped loving him—he's determined that a wedding will take place in the garden nurtured by faith and love.

Where healing flows...

Look for

The Wedding Garden
by Linda Goodnight

Available May 2010
wherever you buy books.

Steeple Hill®

LI87595

REQUEST YOUR FREE BOOKS!

HARLEQUIN®

Blaze™

Red-hot reads!

2 FREE NOVELS PLUS 2 FREE GIFTS!

YES! Please send me 2 FREE Harlequin® Blaze™ novels and my 2 FREE gifts (gifts are worth about $10). After receiving them, if I don't wish to receive any more books, I can return the shipping statement marked "cancel." If I don't cancel, I will receive 6 brand-new novels every month and be billed just $4.24 per book in the U.S. or $4.71 per book in Canada. That's a saving of at least 15% off the cover price. It's quite a bargain. Shipping and handling is just 50¢ per book.* I understand that accepting the 2 free books and gifts places me under no obligation to buy anything. I can always return a shipment and cancel at any time. Even if I never buy another book, the two free books and gifts are mine to keep forever.

151/351 HDN E5LS

Name	(PLEASE PRINT)
Address	Apt. #
City	State/Prov.	Zip/Postal Code

Signature (if under 18, a parent or guardian must sign)

Mail to the Harlequin Reader Service:
IN U.S.A.: P.O. Box 1867, Buffalo, NY 14240-1867
IN CANADA: P.O. Box 609, Fort Erie, Ontario L2A 5X3

Not valid for current subscribers to Harlequin Blaze books.

**Want to try two free books from another line?
Call 1-800-873-8635 or visit www.morefreebooks.com.**

* Terms and prices subject to change without notice. Prices do not include applicable taxes. N.Y. residents add applicable sales tax. Canadian residents will be charged applicable provincial taxes and GST. Offer not valid in Quebec. This offer is limited to one order per household. All orders subject to approval. Credit or debit balances in a customer's account(s) may be offset by any other outstanding balance owed by or to the customer. Please allow 4 to 6 weeks for delivery. Offer available while quantities last.

Your Privacy: Harlequin Books is committed to protecting your privacy. Our Privacy Policy is available online at www.eHarlequin.com or upon request from the Reader Service. From time to time we make our lists of customers available to reputable third parties who may have a product or service of interest to you. If you would prefer we not share your name and address, please check here. ☐

Help us get it right—We strive for accurate, respectful and relevant communications. To clarify or modify your communication preferences, visit us at www.ReaderService.com/consumerschoice.

HB10R